Praise for Jenny Hale

"Jenny Hale writes touching, beautiful stories."—***New York Times* bestselling author RaeAnne Thayne**

"A festive addition to the Holiday romance genre with a subtle poignancy that sets it apart."—***Kirkus Reviews*** on *The Noel Bridge*

"I can always count on Jenny Hale to sweep me away with her heartwarming romantic tales."—**bestselling author Denise Hunter** on *Butterfly Sisters*

One of "19 Dreamy Summer Romances to Whisk You Away" in ***Oprah Magazine*** on *The Summer House*

One of "24 Dreamy Books about Romance" in ***Oprah Daily*** on *The Summer House*

Included in "Beach Reads Perfect for Summer" in ***Southern Living Magazine*** on *The Beach House*

"Touching, fun-filled, and redolent with salt air and the fragrance of summer, this seaside tale is a perfect volume for most romance collections."—***Library Journal*** on *The Summer House*

"Hale's impeccably executed contemporary romance is the perfect gift for readers who love sweetly romantic love stories imbued with all the warmth and joy of the holiday season."—***Booklist*** on *Christmas Wishes and Mistletoe Kisses*

"A great summer beach read."—***PopSugar*** on *Summer at Firefly Beach*

"Hale's prose evokes the magic of the Outer Banks... A breezy romance as satisfying as ice cream on the beach."—***Kirkus Reviews*** on *The Summer Hideaway*

Also by Jenny Hale

The Broken Hearts Beach Club

Where Are You Now

Out of the Blue

The Summer Hideaway

The Golden Hour

The Magic of Sea Glass

Butterfly Sisters

The Memory Keeper

Ten Christmases Without You

The Noel Bridge

Meet Me at Christmas

The Christmas Letters

Postmarked December

Postmarked December

JENNY HALE

USA TODAY BESTSELLING AUTHOR

HARPETH ROAD PRESS®

Nashville

HARPETH ROAD PRESS

Published by Harpeth Road Press (USA)
P.O. Box 158184
Nashville, TN 37215

Paperback: 978-1-963483-60-4
eBook: 978-1-963483-59-8
Library of Congress Control Number: 2026913780

Postmarked December: An Inspirational, Emotional Christmas Escape

Cover Design by Kristen Ingebretson
Cover Images © Shutterstock, Adobe, Depositphotos

Harpeth Road Press, October 2026

Chapter One

December 17th

Heather Hart sat cross-legged and motionless on the sofa under a large-weave holiday-red blanket. She was barely aware of the glistening Christmas tree in the corner, the falling snow outside her Nashville apartment window, or the dwindling fire. Her entire attention was on the television. Through the blur of tears, a carefree version of herself that she no longer recognized ran down the beach, giggling and hiking up her chiffon gown. Her long brown hair blew in the coastal wind, and her newlywed husband, Toby, trailed behind her, laughing.

The water was bright blue, the sand pearly under their feet. The golden sun beamed down on them, creating a dreamy glow—a stark contrast to the gray December sky outside Heather's apartment. Toby had his arms stretched out, sprinting after her, barefoot, in his gray suit with a pink-rose boutonniere. They ran off-screen, leaving her wedding bouquet visible in the sand. She waited for the waves to overwhelm the bundle of roses and carry the bouquet out to sea. In reality, it hadn't happened, but if that video had mirrored their future, it should have.

Her phone rang, yanking her from the memory. She tensed, but didn't leave the sofa, and it eventually stopped.

Reporters had somehow gotten her personal number and had been calling her, off and on, ever since Toby's song "Only the Sound," released after his death, had become a worldwide number-one single. It had topped the streaming and radio charts with over 2.1 billion global streams, and the album, *Make Me Whole Again*, had dominated the year-end charts with over 3.26 million album sales and 6.97 million equivalent album units by December. It was Toby's album of a lifetime. And he wasn't there to see the full fruition of his success.

Because of Toby's rapid decline, and the fact that so few details were released about it, the press was also still trying to get a handle on what had happened to him. Always opting for charity missions over world tours and awards shows, Toby had stayed out of the public eye as much as possible, so it seemed to the public that his death had literally come out of nowhere.

The holiday season was picking up, so the calls had as well —all of the callers wanting to be the first to break the story about his cancer and his bittersweet rise to success, given the album's recent achievements. Heather hadn't spoken to a single one, nor was she planning to. She and Toby had decided that together when the early sales numbers had come in. He'd wanted nothing to do with accolades, big venues, or reporters. And she'd given him her solemn promise that she would not give in to their pressure.

Toby had been an incredibly private person. He was protective of Heather, suggesting she keep and use her maiden name, Matthews, as her legal name, to prevent people from knowing who she was on legal documents. That was fine with her, but she called herself Heather Hart. And despite his fame, he had no social media, which was also fine with her. She didn't either. When his cancer had taken hold, she was glad to be able to easily cut off from the outside world without the noise of everyone checking in. Because of the care he'd taken to preserve her privacy, and the fact that neither of them was terribly flashy, no one seemed to recognize her when she was out.

Toby always saw discretion as a sign of respect and humility, believing some things should remain unshared with the public. It seemed almost fitting that he wasn't there for most of his worldwide success. He wouldn't have known how to handle it. Recognition was a side effect of doing what he loved, which was strumming his guitar and jotting down songs in his battered notebook, giving his life a melody.

Now, Heather couldn't ask him what to do or who to talk to, so out of an abiding regard for his wishes and a need to hold onto him, she avoided all the press. That was what he would've wanted anyway.

Her phone rang for a second time.

The distraction from her wedding video was probably a good thing. It being only early in the morning of the first day of her Christmas break, she'd already been struggling, wondering how she'd ever make it through this first Christmas without Toby.

She'd been looking for the box of memories that held her favorite photo of them, a rare appearance at his publisher's holiday gala two years ago. That had been one of the memories she held onto the most.

❄

Toby hung his guitar on the wall mount behind the sofa, his songwriting notebook and pencil, along with balled-up pieces of paper, still strewn across the coffee table. "I bought you something."

Heather marked her place in her book with a finger and

looked up, curious. Toby showed his love by doing rather than buying, so she was unsure of his motives.

He walked across the room and removed the book from her lap, turning it over on the table to keep her place. Then he took her hands and gently pulled her to a standing position.

"I know I'm the one who doesn't like the limelight," he said. "And I haven't taken you out like I should have."

"It's fine, really, Toby. I married you, so I knew what I was getting into," she teased.

He offered that adorable grin. Then he leaned down and kissed her. "You deserve to sparkle like the bright star you are. I RSVPed to Stargate's gala."

She widened her eyes dramatically. "You? You're going to your publisher's gala?"

"No press allowed," he said, his eyebrows bobbing. "Just me... And you..." He let go of one of her hands and spun her around. "And this..."

He led her into the bedroom. Hanging on the closet door was a long red silk-and-chiffon designer gown she'd admired when they'd been in New York.

She gasped. "Is that the Iris Acatrinei gown?"

"Mm-hm. And I can't wait to see you in it. And later, out of it." He tickled her sides, and she squealed with laughter.

❄

During moments when he'd still felt good, Toby had been organizing their paperwork, getting all their accounts ready for her to take over, and putting boxes of old files in storage while she was at work, sending them with a hired courier. She just knew he'd inadvertently sent the box of photos with their gala picture in it on one of those storage runs. When she couldn't find it, she'd put on the video instead. Why she'd decided to watch it during the holidays was beyond her. Masochistic, really.

When Heather's phone rang for the third time, she clicked off the television. She rubbed her eyelids to dry the remaining tears and pushed the blanket off her legs. Clearing her throat, she crossed the room to the kitchen counter to get her phone and check the calls. She blew out a sigh of relief to see the latest was her fellow librarian and best friend, Marion Wilkins.

"Just checking in on my favorite person on her first day of Christmas break," Marion's chipper voice bellowed down the line.

They'd worked together in the Ellis Elementary library for a year now and, both personally and professionally, Heather couldn't have managed a day without her. With Toby's music career exploding, she hadn't had to hold a job. Toby gave a huge portion of their earnings to charitable causes, leaving them just what they needed to live on, which had always been perfectly fine with her. And then, she needed something to take her mind off the stress of his cancer. So she'd made use of her Master's of Education and Library Science degrees and taken the job at Ellis Elementary School. Since then, Marion had been with her through all the highs and lows.

"Wait. What was that?"

Heather held her breath and sharpened her hearing. "What was what?"

"Did I hear a sniffle? Your nose sounds stuffy."

She faked a cough. "I might be coming down with something."

"Heather… You okay?"

"I'm fine. Really." She forced another cough.

"I'm coming over," Marion said. "I'll pack a bag in case the roads get bad and I can't get back home. Be there in twenty minutes with two coffees and a sack of obscene carbohydrates."

"I might be sick, remember? Sniffling..." The drive over was not ideal on the slick roads and, given the early and unpredictable snow-and-ice mix, the route was sure to be treacherous. The last thing she wanted was her poor friend to have to trudge outside in the icy mess because Heather couldn't keep her emotions in check.

"You're not sick. Your cough doesn't sound like that."

"You don't have to come," Heather said. "What about Anthony? You don't want to leave him stranded in the snow."

Marion and her husband Anthony had been having marital problems. Marion had said, more than once, that she didn't want to burden Heather with her "drama," given what Heather had been through, so her friend had been tight-lipped about the situation.

"He's a big boy. He'll probably enjoy a night without me jabbering away. And he'll have Scarlett to keep him company."

An image surfaced of the calico kitten Marion and Anthony had gotten a few months ago that they'd named after the heroine in *Gone with the Wind*. Marion had thought the shared responsibility might give her and Anthony common ground, something positive to focus on apart from their troubles. Scarlett was a little ball of purring fur and so adorable that Heather almost asked her to bring it, but she didn't have a litter box.

"Walking through your door in twenty," Marion said.

"See you soon." Heather ended the call, stuck her phone in her pocket, and ran her fingers under her eyes.

Heather actually hoped Marion would get snowed in with her because that would be the best thing that could happen. She needed someone to yank the remote from her hand, shake her by the shoulders, and force her to think about anything other than the fact that she wasn't even thirty yet and already a widow.

This first Christmas break without Toby was harder than

she'd thought it would be. He was the one who'd anchored her holiday. He'd always done all the cooking, but when Christmas came around he really shined. He found time in the kitchen to be both creative and calming, so they had a never-ending stream of delectable dishes and baked goods. He also put up a freshly cut tree each year and played Christmas music on his guitar, constantly. Without him this season, the silence was deafening.

A Nashville songwriter and musician, Toby had always been everywhere. He'd written for quite a few big names in music, and his songs played in every restaurant and honky-tonk in the country. But this year, that was especially the case. With the success of *Make Me Whole Again*, his Christmas album played relentlessly in all the shops and cafés, so she hadn't wanted to leave her apartment.

The final cut of his record the September before last had been the last celebration he could muster, before he'd gotten too sick to go out. Knowing what was ahead of him, he'd teased her and told her he'd rather be sick than attend a gala.

And then there was the press. Luckily, in Nashville, people left her alone, but with his death, his songwriting and incredible acts of charity came to light, and people realized his talent both behind the scenes and as a performer. His fans across the globe wanted to know the details about his rapid decline in health, and national magazines and news programs were all too eager to oblige. She'd endured countless online conspiracies before he died: that he'd given up his career, that he'd assumed a new identity, and that he was penniless—those were the big ones.

Already this season, she'd had calls from a few magazines, the local news, and a couple of independent reporters, but she hadn't called them back. Toby had said he didn't want anyone to focus on the thing that took him, but rather, to remember him by his music.

Heather folded the blanket she'd been covering up with and placed it on the edge of the sofa. She'd gotten the red blanket for Toby when he'd really started to get sick.

Toby hadn't known he had cancer until it was stage 4. From there, it had progressed quickly. Not a fan of conventional medicine, he'd tried everything—fasting, experimental drugs, natural remedies—but his recovery wasn't in the cards. He had moments where he'd get bursts of energy, and they'd talk for a few hours, but most of the time he slept.

❄

"A friend of mine—remember Stone, the guy we saw at the bar last summer who was so funny?" Toby seemed to struggle even to swallow, his lips chapped and dry.

"Yeah?" She put his water cup on the tray by his bed.

"He has a kid at Ellis Elementary," he said, his eyes bobbing shut. "He called to see how I was when you were in the shower."

"You answered the phone?" she worried aloud.

"It's my only diversion these days." He forced a smile. "But he made small talk about..."

For an instant, she thought he'd fallen asleep midsentence, but he opened his eyes and continued.

"...nothing at all. It was torture." He tried to smile again at her and make eye contact. Those eyes that had looked at her with so much love were yellow and fading. "They said his daughter hadn't returned her library book when she had. It came out that they're shorthanded, so his wife's been volunteering. They're struggling to find a long-term sub for the librarian on maternity leave."

She nodded, unsure of where he was going with that.

"You always wanted to work in a library, and you need to

do something outside of caring for me," he said as she draped the new red blanket across his legs.

"Why would I want to get a job right now?" she asked.

He lifted a weak hand. "Because doing this sucks."

"I'm not going to leave you," she said.

"I have a nurse. We can up her hours."

"What if people realize I'm your wife? Will that make things crazy for the kids? I wouldn't want to turn the school into a circus."

"I doubt anyone would give you trouble."

He was probably right. They wanted to see him, not her. "I don't know..."

"Do it for me. You need to go out and feel the world because I can't anymore."

❄

So in the middle of the biggest crisis in her life, she'd taken the library job. While she was at work, he slept, and when he was awake in the wee hours of the morning, she could barely keep her eyes open. She knew, then, it could be their last Christmas, so she took whatever he could give with gratitude.

Friends and industry folks would stop by, but when December rolled around she'd asked if they could refrain, due to the spread of germs. That was when things got really quiet.

The slower pace had given her and Toby a little time to come to terms with what they were facing, and they never shied away from it. They talked about the end.

❄

"If at all possible, I'll be here with you after I leave this planet," he said one night as they brushed their teeth, before he'd gotten too sick to get out of bed. "But not in a psycho way." The edge of his lip twitched upward with his amusement. "Like if you end up dating someone, I'll probably hang out downtown or something." He made a disgusted face, and she laughed.

"Don't talk about me dating," she said. "That's weird."

His face became serious. He set his toothbrush on the edge of the sink and took her arm, turning her toward him. "No, it isn't. The very last thing I'd want for you is to go through your life alone. You have my absolute blessing."

Tears welled up and she shook her head. He pulled her in, and she buried her face in his chest.

He pulled back to look at her. "Shoot, if I could pick him myself, I would." His gaze became unsteady, as if he were thinking about something important, but he didn't say anything else and she was too afraid to ask.

"Just promise you'll come back if you can," she said through the lump in her throat.

"Promise." He leaned down and kissed her.

❄

They'd prayed together and had long talks about their faith. She believed he'd live on after he left this world. And she trusted him to be true to his word. If at all possible, he'd be there for her.

But she had yet to see any sign of him.

Chapter Two

With Marion probably minutes away, Heather went into the bathroom to take stock of her pink nose, the dark circles under her eyes, and her generally disheveled appearance. Her skin was pasty. Her brown eyes were clouded and bloodshot, and her dark locks were dulled; she hadn't gone to the salon in ages. Her appearance was a far cry from that wedding video. Now, she felt frumpy and out of touch entirely with style. With an audible exhale, she turned on the cold water, splashing some on her face, happy that Marion had insisted on coming over.

Marion knew her better than anyone, which was why she'd called, certainly. She'd guessed that Heather would be wallowing on her first day off. Heather didn't manage time off well anymore because during that time she should be managing the leftover affairs that fell into her lap after Toby's death. He was an only child, and his parents were older when they had him, and they, too, had passed on. So everything fell on her shoulders.

She hadn't looked at his contracts to reconcile his percentages and check the money coming in, at what point she'd get the rights to his old songs, or how much he should be getting paid and when. She took the publisher at its word. There was also that storage unit full of their old files. He'd been doing weird things at the end, his medicine making him forgetful, but arguing with her and telling her he could manage. Out of exhaustion and love, she'd let him, figuring she could always go through the storage unit later. There was also their vacation cabin that she still hadn't located the key to. She hadn't seen it since he'd had contractors in to make upgrades to it.

Their accountant had been managing the company that kept it running, as well as their taxes, and she needed to get in contact with him to make sure she was in the know with their accounts. There was so much to do, but almost a year later, she still couldn't bring herself to take care of any of it. She just let others run it all.

Wiping her face, she took another deep breath and looked around. "Toby? Can you hear me up there?" she called out.

Given his current state, promises or not, if he could reach her, would he really want to spend his time down here in this small, cold bathroom?

"It's okay if you want to hang out up there," she said. "I'm crying, but I'll be all right. I know you never loved this apartment." He'd thought it could do with more security, but she'd adored the wide-open floor plan, the high ceilings, and the view of the Nashville skyline, so he'd relented. "Even if you *are* able to somehow stick your head in and say hello, you don't have to."

While she secretly yearned to see some miraculous appearance, there was another part of her that hoped he'd let go of all this down here. He didn't need to worry about her. He had eternity ahead of him. She wanted to be strong for him, and most of the time, she could manage. But some days were harder than others.

Her phone rang again. She checked the number. Not

recognizing it, she let it go to voicemail. When the message showed, she listened to it.

"Hi, Heather. I'm hoping we can meet. Toby's album is up for an award—"

She'd already heard. It was up for album of the year. While she'd always wanted to get dressed up and go to one of those awards shows, she and Toby never had. He'd promised her they were more hype than excitement.

"It's lots of long hours sitting and smiling awkwardly at half-baked jokes with people at your table, when the actual people you want to sit with are so far across the room that you never even see them," he'd said. *"If you want to celebrate, let's have a party, and I'll eat the food I want, with the friends I want, and have zero bathroom lines."*

She deleted the message, but then noticed she'd missed another one, so she hit play.

"Hi, Heather, this is Alice Beckmeyer with Stargate Publishing here in Nashville. I was going through our records for something else, and I happened upon an inquiry about four months ago. We had a call for a last-minute request from someone who's written something about Toby and needed to double-check their copyright information for a couple of his songs with us before it's distributed. I didn't speak to them, our legal department did, and they said they'd cleared everything, but I thought I'd give you a heads-up that something might be released soon. I know Toby wouldn't be thrilled about that..."

She'd have to call Alice back after the holiday and thank her for the warning. She couldn't face it now. The press was relentless—they always seemed to have so much to say about Toby, yet they didn't know a thing. No one knew their real story of love and endurance during his sickness, of how he'd invested all his available money into helping the less fortunate, or the way he'd told Heather he adored her when it was just the two of them. And she would keep it that way. If she could do one thing for Toby, it would be to live the way he'd wanted—privately.

Heather was so thankful for Marion. She needed a good coffee and a jolt back to the present. She dug around in her makeup bin, grabbed her best concealer, and swiped it under her dark eyes. Then she used a little sponge and patted it until the last of the redness on her rims had disappeared. She moved on to powder and blush. When the color made her look more human, she combed her hair and took a step back to check her reflection. She'd hidden most of her sadness.

Just as she'd tidied the living room and wiped down the kitchen, Marion was at the door with a duffel bag on her shoulder, a tray with two coffees, and a small paper sack.

"I went five minutes out of the way to The Steaming Quill," her friend said.

"Oooh, that's my favorite." Heather let her inside.

"I know. That's why I went." She crossed the room, dropped her bag on the floor with an odd clinking sound, and set the coffees on the bar that separated the small kitchen from the living area. Then she began digging around in the sack. "I got their hazelnut-ganache-stuffed croissants, lemon-lavender scones, and salted caramel butter bread."

Heather rolled her eyes in ecstasy as she took the lid off her coffee to reveal the foamy heart and a rich scent of maple and brown sugar—absolute decadence. "What would I do without you?"

"Probably consume something healthier than this." Marion laughed at her own joke. She washed her hands and then helped herself to a plate from the cabinet. She arranged the pastries artfully. "You look better than I expected." She pushed the plate toward Heather.

"I needed you to call," Heather finally admitted. "Knowing you were on the way helped."

Marion gave her a squeeze. "I had a feeling."

"It's just this time of year..." Heather tried not to slip back into the low place she'd been in a few minutes ago. "I don't even know how to do the holidays without him. What eats at me the most is that Toby and I had our whole lives ahead of us. What was the purpose of his gift of singing if he couldn't see it through?"

"He has the number-one song this year."

"I know. But think about where his career could've gone."

Like everything he touched, his Christmas album released last year turned to gold. One of the songs, "Christmas With You," flew up the charts a few years ago, and had been a cult favorite ever since.

"I feel like the cancer stole his happy ending—and mine."

"It did," Marion said. "And he was robbed. But your life is still going. There *are* more endings out there for you. You just have to grab another one when you feel strong enough."

"You make moving on sound easy." Heather took a drink of the warm, nutty coffee.

"I doubt it's easy, but maybe it will be smoother if you relax and let life happen. Don't try so hard to plan it."

"I'm a librarian. Planning is my thing."

"Have you forgotten that I, also, am in your field of work?" Marion took a croissant and tore it in two, the chocolate center whipped and fluffy. She offered half to Heather.

Heather wrinkled her nose. "I've never understood how you ended up enjoying library science, given the way you are."

"The way *I am*?" Marion nibbled her end of the croissant.

"You oversleep. You never know what day it is. You're disorganized. That's not a cut-down; they're your own words."

"Mmm, but I love a good book," she cooed. "And you, missy"—she waggled a finger—"aren't any better than I am. You don't know how to bake for yourself."

She shrugged. "Toby always cooked."

"It's *reading*. You just read the recipe."

Heather laughed. Happiness felt good.

"Speaking of books..." Marion took Heather by the arm and led her to her overnight bag. She put the croissant between her teeth and unzipped the duffel, the clinking sound returning. With a flourish, she retrieved a brown leather journal and held it out. Removing the pastry from her lips, she said, "I got this for you. Merry Christmas."

"You didn't have to get me anything."

They'd already exchanged gift cards at work.

"I know, but I think this might be good for you. You could write down your feelings. You do better when you express them, so on the days you have no one to talk to, you can write."

Leave it to Marion to fill the void once more.

Heather leaned in and gave her best friend a hug. "Thank you."

"Of course."

"What else is in your bag, by the way?" Heather asked. "Something keeps tinkling."

"Oh, that's my other gift—to both of us." She pulled out two bottles of rosé. "In case the snow doesn't let up. We can binge-watch Christmas movies and drink wine until we fall asleep."

"I thought you weren't a planner," Heather teased.

"Wine, caffeine, and sugar are a whole different story. And I already had the rosé at the house."

"Fair enough."

Heather brought the plate of pastries over to the coffee table, placing them next to her new journal, and she and Marion settled in with their drinks. Heather would never have gotten through the holiday without her. As she sipped her deliciously festive latte, she couldn't deny how much hope her friend had brought to her life. So much so that Marion had her believing that maybe things could get better.

She could start by continuing the life she'd begun—for Toby. If he were here, what would he want for Christmas this year? Without a future with him, his potential answer was hard to know. What did *she* want? The truth was, she wanted a little of Toby to show up, and that was probably the issue. She had a new life to live. She also wanted to be happy—something she couldn't be without him.

Her gaze fell on the journal. Maybe she could use it to document this new life—the wins and losses. She'd make it a love letter to Toby, writing to him about what she was going through. She might find a slip of light in her darkness to hold onto, and maybe, if she was lucky, a stroke of Christmas magic.

Chapter Three

"How many movies did we end up watching last night?" Heather asked, running her fingers through her hair as she sat next to Marion on the sofa.

The skin between Marion's brows wrinkled. "I lost track by glass four."

Yesterday afternoon had begun with card games and long talks. Even though the snow hadn't impacted the roads, Marion had decided to stay. By dinner, they'd ordered a pizza. Then the wine was opened and their movie marathon began.

Now, the half-empty pizza box sat next to the remnants of stale pastries and cloudy glasses on the distressed iron coffee table Toby had picked out for its substantial size and organic feel. Heather had usually softened it with fresh flowers, but over the last year, she hadn't bothered.

She yawned and got up to peer out the window at the skyline. A thin blanket of white surrounded them, and the city had slowed to a quiet hum.

"This cold snap is a surprise," she said.

The drop in temperatures had collided with the perfect

storm to give them actual snow at the holidays, something Nashville hadn't seen too often in Christmases past. While the total amount of snow wasn't much to write home about, it was enough to put her in a festive mood. And she couldn't help but think of Toby.

"Too bad the storm didn't come in last year," she said, wishing he could've seen it. "Toby loved Christmas."

Marion gave her a sad smile.

Heather didn't allow herself to think about how little he'd have appreciated the winter scene at that stage of his illness. But it would've been nice to roll his bed to the window, even if only for a few minutes.

The phone rang. Heather disregarded it.

"The coffee's in the pantry," she said, pulling down two mugs from the cabinet above the sink.

Marion helped herself to the bag of coffee and began scooping grounds into the filter basket of the coffeemaker as the phone continued to ring. "You gonna get that?" she asked.

Heather eyed the caller. "It's an unknown number." She handed the mugs to Marion, then filled the carafe with water and dumped it into the machine.

When her phone finally stopped ringing, she swiped up to clear the notification, but paused. There was a message. "Let me just make sure this isn't something important." She opened the screen, hit play, and put the phone to her ear.

"Hello, this is Anderson Miller with *Nashville News Tonight*. I was wondering if I could ask you a few questions about your late husband. We'd love to do a story on his life and work. If you could give me a call back at this number at your earliest convenience, that would be great. Congratulations, by the way, on the success of the album this year and the number one spot for 'Christmas With You'—"

She ended the call.

"Anything interesting?" Marion slid a mug of coffee her way.

Heather set the phone on the counter. "Another reporter." She sucked in a breath, went over to the fridge, and took out the cream. "I have no idea how they were able to get my number, but everyone seems to have it." She handed the cream to Marion, who topped off her mug, as Heather's mind went to what might happen when they went back to work after Christmas. Would people find out her place of employment and try to contact her there?

"Nothing's private these days. It's amazing how they can find that stuff out." Marion stirred her coffee.

"Yeah..."

The coffeemaker beeped to alert that it was set to warming.

Marion came up beside her. "You look concerned. What's going on in that head of yours?"

"'Christmas With You' is number one again this year, apparently." She climbed onto the small barstool next to Marion and slumped over her mug. "I should be thrilled, but it just reminds me of what I've lost. I have zero holiday joy."

Marion put an arm around her. "Start by appreciating the little moments—baby steps." She patted Heather's back. "Maybe delight in a couple of nice dinners with friends and then a Christmas card or two. Slowly, you can build up to full-on holiday joy."

"Speaking of Christmas cards, I haven't checked my mailbox downstairs in two days. It's probably overflowing."

"Go check it then. If you find me a pan and a few eggs, I'll make us some breakfast."

Glad Marion was there to bounce her feelings off of, Heather gave her a squeeze. "Thank you." She pulled a pan from one of the bottom cabinets and got out the eggs, bread, and butter. "I'll be right back."

Marion blew her a kiss.

When Heather returned, Marion had set them each a place on the oversized table that seated eight. When Heather bought it, she'd hoped to give her and Toby an opportunity to entertain smaller groups without having to use the dining space, but they hadn't gotten the chance to do that.

Marion had lit the candle between their settings. *How thoughtful.*

Heather lumped the mail onto the counter while Marion set her mug by one of the plates.

"How can I help with breakfast?" Heather asked.

"I've got it. Scrambled eggs and toast aren't exactly culinary enigmas."

Heather chuckled and started sifting through the mail. "Toby used to do all the cooking, so I never really learned how. I probably should've gotten him to teach me a few recipes." She ripped up a credit-card solicitation. "He used to make this meatloaf casserole that was out of this world. I used to make him cook batches of it so I could give them as housewarming and new-baby gifts. It doesn't sound like much from the title, but it was delicious."

"You don't have the recipe written down?" Marion asked, untwisting the bread tie.

"Sadly, no. He was one of those people who just threw things together."

Marion dropped two pieces of bread into the toaster.

"So much junk," Heather said, setting a car insurance flyer on the trash pile she was making. "And not even the good junk. Remember when we used to get those sales catalogs during the holidays? My grandma got them every year, and we'd pick out what we wanted for Christmas. Did you ever get those in the mail?"

Marion shook her head, holding her mug with both

hands. "I just wrote three or four things on a sticky note and handed it to my mom."

Heather laughed. "Why doesn't that surprise me?" She set her electric bill to the side, then continued opening and discarding various mailers.

When the toast popped, Marion plated a piece for each of them and dished up their eggs. As she returned the plates to the table, Heather's progress slowed. In her hand was a red-and-white envelope with a dark green seal.

Marion craned her neck to see it as she retrieved the butter. "That's a pretty envelope. Who's it from?"

"I'm not sure. There's no return address." She squinted at the postmark. "It's marked Franklin, Tennessee." She opened the envelope as she racked her brain for possible friends who lived twenty-five minutes' drive from her in the lovely little town of Franklin.

Inside wasn't a card but a single sheet of paper. She read the message.

> While "Christmas With You" is my favorite holiday song, I'd rather sing "All I Want for Christmas is You." Got a corkscrew ready? Let's have ourselves a bottle of wine. Go get us another. You know where to go. Merry Christmas.

Heather froze, the note falling to the floor.

"You okay?" Marion rushed to her side.

Tears sprang to Heather's eyes at the memory: two Christmases ago, Toby yanking her into his arms while Mariah Carey played too loudly over the speaker in their apartment. They'd been out to dinner with friends and had too much wine, and he'd insisted on having more. They'd bought a bottle of Tennessee blackberry wine when they were shopping in Franklin, and she'd saved it to gift someone the next time they went to a party.

"Let's open it," he urged, giving her a spin.

"No." She giggled. "It's for a special occasion."

"There's no better occasion than this!" He dipped her as the music pulsed around them. He pressed his lips to hers, neither of them having any idea of what they'd face the next year.

"You're white as a ghost. Do you need to sit?" Marion said.

Heather didn't move.

Marion picked up the sheet of paper and studied it. "Who wrote this?"

Tears streamed down Heather's cheeks. "I have no idea."

Surely Toby couldn't come back to me to help me through Christmas... Could he? That's just silly. But it was the first thing to come to mind. Heather mustered the strength to address Marion again.

"The message reads as if it's from Toby. He'd be the only one to know these things. Could this be some kind of prank?"

"Is it his handwriting?" Marion asked.

Heather scrutinized it. "It could be. It's hard to say." It had been so long since he'd been able to write legibly, and his notebooks were full of rushed, scratched-down lyrics, that she couldn't remember what his handwriting looked like when he took time and tried. It sort of looked like his old writing. She dared not believe that it was.

"Maybe it was a well-meaning but poorly executed gesture?" Marion wrinkled her nose, concern written on her face. "Or could someone have been holding it for him and mailed it just now?"

Heather didn't answer. She was too busy studying the envelope. Franklin was where they'd bought that wine. And the post date was two days ago. Had anyone seen them buy the wine two years prior? Certainly not. They'd gone in through the back door, and the owner had secured the shop. No one knew about that night—she hadn't even told Marion. How could anyone have known? She took the letter from her friend and peered down at it through the haze of tears.

"If he did get someone to send it, why would he send *this* message to me? Why would he randomly want me to have a bottle of wine?"

Marion shrugged, looking perplexed. "Maybe he thought you might need it?"

Heather tried to make sense of the note, but *nothing* made sense. Her mind was a muddle. She dared not consider that she'd actually thought about what he'd want for Christmas this year, and what she'd want... Was it his gift? As much as she'd hoped for it, there was no way he could answer her... Right?

She pulled the envelope open to make sure there wasn't something she'd missed, but nothing else was inside. There was no return address of any kind.

Fighting off the feeling of lightheadedness, she recounted to Marion the story of that night with Toby and the wine, explaining that they'd been inside—just the two of them—when they'd had the wine, and no one had seen them.

The memory was too good, too happy, and she broke down.

"Do you have some kind of stalker in the apartment?" Marion rubbed her back and gazed around the room protectively, scanning the ceiling and walls.

"I feel nauseous." Heather hiccupped, the tears still flowing.

"Should we call the police?" Marion went over to the window and looked both ways down the street.

"They probably wouldn't do anything. No harm's been done, apart from tearing my heart out." She carefully folded the letter, returned it to the envelope, and set it on the counter. Then she went into the bathroom and wiped her tears from her cheeks, trying to get herself together.

"What a weird thing to do to someone," Marion said, squinting at the envelope when she returned. "We should at least try to figure out if it's malicious."

"It doesn't say to meet anyone or to do anything, apart from buy myself a bottle of wine."

"Unless they'll be waiting at the wine shop." Marion gasped and rubbed her hands together, showing her unease. "What if the paper's laced with something? We could both be contaminated."

"Well, the door's locked, so no one can attack us, and I feel fine. How do you feel?"

"Woozy, suddenly." Marion went to the sink and washed her hands. "I'm feeling dizzy."

"Are you really, or do you just think you are?"

"I'm having trouble getting a deep breath." Drying her hands on the kitchen towel, she walked over to Heather and breathed into her face. "Am I wheezing?" She ogled the envelope on the counter.

"No, you sound fine." Heather couldn't help herself. She started laughing and half crying at Marion's obvious panic over nothing.

"Even if it isn't laced, it's still bizarre."

"Yeah, I know. Why don't I call the Franklin post office? It was postmarked two days ago, and it's pretty unique with the wax seal. Maybe someone remembers who sent it?"

"Good idea."

Heather stared at her cold eggs. Did she want to know who'd mailed her that cryptic message? Or did she want to live for a little while in the irrational hope that it was a nod from Toby?

Chapter Four

With their breakfast stone-cold on the table in the kitchen, the candle still flickering between the plates, Heather and Marion sat together on the sofa with the phone leaning against the empty vase on the coffee table. Heather squeezed Marion's hand while the phone pulsed.

"Hello, Franklin Post Office. How may I direct your call?"

Heather leaned forward. "Um. I live in Nashville, and I received a letter. I think someone mailed it from your post office a couple days ago. There's no return address or signature, so I was calling to see if you all knew who mailed it."

The woman on the other end of the line offered a cheerful chuckle. "Ma'am, we get so much mail coming through our office each day. It's hard to know."

"Please," Heather pleaded. "It's really important. The envelope is red and white, and it has a green wax seal with a Christmas tree."

"It's the holidays. We get a ton of those."

"I'm sure you do, but the note inside wasn't signed, and it

had a pretty unique message. I really need to figure out who sent it. Could you at least ask someone, humor me?"

A warmhearted sigh came down the line. "When did you say it was mailed?"

"Two days ago."

"Let me see who was working. Hold on just a minute."

Marion burst into a smile and pumped her fist.

After a pause, a clatter on the other end of the line drew their attention back to the call. "Hello?" a different voice said. "This wouldn't be, by chance, someone named *Heather*, would it?"

Heather and Marion locked wide eyes, and a tingle of anticipation swam through Heather's veins. "Yes."

"I can't believe you actually called. I've been hoping you'd call." She huffed out a laugh of disbelief. "A man showed up with an envelope about the size of a Christmas card. He said if anyone came in asking about it, it would probably be someone named Heather. And he insisted that I write down a message and keep it for a couple of weeks. I'm supposed to tell you to go to the wine shop downtown. It's called Bottle and Barrel. Do you know it?"

Her skin went cold. Bottle and Barrel was the wine shop where she and Toby bought the bottle of wine two years ago. And the note had said to get another bottle. *You know where to go...*

"Yeah," she said, her mouth dry. What was going on? "What am I supposed to do at the wine shop?"

"He didn't say," the woman replied. "I thought you'd know."

So she had to buy a bottle of wine? Why? "What did the man look like?" she asked.

"Tall, dark hair, kind smile."

Those were Toby's characteristics. She swallowed.

They finished the call, and Heather stared at the phone, her mind racing.

"What could be at that wine shop?" Heather asked, more to herself than Marion.

"Probably the stalker," Marion said.

Heather blinked to get her thoughts together. "What if it isn't? What if it's... something else?" Her need to fill the emptiness Toby had left overcame her. Perhaps it was the magic of the holiday season, but she had a strange feeling she was meant to find out. "I need to go see."

"Well, you're not going alone." Marion checked the time. "It's ten. Think a wine shop is open that early?"

"I don't know," Heather replied. "But we could walk around and shop until it opens."

"Shopping?" Marion's posture lifted. "Anthony's at work all day. We can take my car."

With a fizzle of hope that she hadn't felt in a very long time, Heather jumped up. "I'll throw on some clothes and brush my teeth." She blew out the candle in the kitchen and ran into her bedroom, where she stripped off her pajamas and fumbled around in her closet for her big fuzzy sweater and a pair of jeans. As she ran a comb through her hair and washed her face, that day from long ago ran like a reel in her mind. Toby dropping a wad of cash in the case of a violinist playing carols on the street corner. Heather gripping the paper cup she'd gotten at the local coffee shop. She and Toby strolling around the square boasting a Christmas tree that stretched to the heavens. Toby had planned the outing as a surprise. He was famous for surprises. Given that fact, she couldn't shake the idea that he could be doing something similar now. Although she had no idea how he would be able to pull it off from where he was.

She got herself together within a few minutes and peeked out her bedroom door. The yellow slip of light was still coming from the bathroom down the hall where Marion was getting ready. Heather took another look at herself in her full-length mirror, then spied her new journal on the nightstand.

She fished around in the drawer for a pen and opened her journal to the first page.

Toby,

Today I remembered the day we bought that bottle of wine in Franklin and then that evening when we drank it and danced together in the living room. It feels like a lifetime ago since we danced like that. I'd give anything to have your arms around me. I wonder, sometimes, if I'll ever feel that kind of bliss again. If you can help me from up there, that would be great. Got any pull with the Big Man upstairs? Marion and I are off to solve a mystery that I think you might have initiated.

I'll keep you posted.

She closed the journal and fastened the strap.

"Ready?" Marion called from the living room.

"As ready as I'll ever be!" She grabbed the letter and locked up.

❄

About thirty-five minutes later, she and Marion pulled to a stop along the snowy curb of Bottle and Barrel in downtown Franklin. The fresh garland around the doorframe and picture window was similar to what it had been when Heather and Toby had shopped there. She only remembered because they'd taken a quick selfie out front before sneaking around the back, and the print was somewhere in the box with the photo from the gala. She swallowed, the sight whisking her back to happier times.

"Here we are," Marion said as she turned off the engine.

The hours on the door said they opened at eleven o'clock.

"We have a little over twenty minutes. What should we do?" Marion asked.

"I know a coffee shop, and our breakfast is still sitting in my apartment. Want to get something to eat?"

"That's a great idea."

Heather slid the letter into her handbag, and they got out of the car. She tightened her coat around her as the cold air slithered down her neck, making her shiver. For an instant, the festive feeling brought a sense of normalcy she hadn't experienced in a long time.

Downtown Franklin shimmered with Christmas magic, its shop-lined sidewalks draped in garlands of pine and holiday ribbon, each public door flanked with elaborate Yuletide decor. A group of carolers gathered on the corner of Main Street, their harmonies floating above the chatter of shoppers. The aroma of cinnamon kettle corn drifted from a nearby vendor's cart, making Heather's stomach grumble.

"I could do with a hot chocolate to go along with my breakfast," Marion said, peering into a shop window full of glittering ornaments and hand-lettered signs.

"Mm, that sounds delicious."

They arrived at the coffee shop. Inside, the warmth was a balm to Heather's icy skin. Marion grabbed them each a menu from the stand near the door. They stepped in line and perused the choices.

"They've got biscuits and gravy," Marion said with a groan of delight.

Heather gave an enthusiastic bounce of her eyebrows. “I’m eyeing the cheese grits.”

“If I get the biscuits, I should probably have the scrambled eggs with pimento cheese to go with it.” Marion sucked in a deep breath and then squealed quietly.

As they waited in line, Heather took in her surroundings. Holiday cheer had settled into every corner of the shop. Evergreen garlands wrapped around doorposts, their branches dotted with holly. A wide tree stood near the counter, its ornaments an eclectic mix of vintage ceramic figurines and deep cranberry bows. They stepped up to a counter draped in garlands with a line of mugs displayed on top for the regulars to put in their orders and asked for a quick minute to decide, letting the people behind them go first. A fireplace at one end crackled beneath stockings labeled with the baristas’ names, casting a warm glow across a set of well-used leather armchairs positioned perfectly for conversation. From behind the counter came the comforting hiss of steaming milk, accompanied by the scent of peppermint mochas, and fresh gingerbread cooling on wire racks.

“I’m getting a decadent coffee, I think. Maybe the Peppermint Ribbon Crunch latte,” Heather stated.

“You had a decadent coffee yesterday and you’re having another? I like your style.” Marion put her arm around her. “And you deserve a wonderful holiday.”

“Thank you.”

When it was their turn, they stepped up to the counter and put in their order. They got their coffees and looked for a place to settle in.

“The chairs are open by the fire,” Heather said, walking quickly to grab them.

Marion unwound her scarf and took off her coat, draping it on the chair. “This is lucky,” she said, sitting across from Heather.

"Yeah..." Heather looked around suspiciously. "Everything seems a little too perfect. I get a Christmas letter that sounds like it's from Toby, I come to the most adorable town for the day—with snow falling—and we get these comfy chairs in a busy coffee shop. What's going on?"

"Your luck is changing?" Marion offered.

"Whose luck is ever like this?"

"Well, we do have the stalker who will probably murder us on the way back to the car, so that should even things out." Marion sipped her coffee.

Heather laughed and then sobered. "Thank you for coming today."

"I had to. I'm the one with pepper spray in my bag."

"What if it isn't a stalker?" Heather said, still giggling. "Who could it be? No one was close enough to Toby and me to know the things in that letter."

"Maybe we'll learn more at the wine shop."

Their names were called and Marion went up to get their breakfasts. They balanced their plates on their laps while basking in the warmth of the fireplace.

"It's nice to get out of the city for a little while." Heather took a bite. The warm, cheesy, slightly sweet corn flavors were simple but delicious, reminding her of home cooking. "Since Toby passed, I don't know what I'm supposed to do with my free time. In better days, the two of us kept each other busy, and then, once he was sick, my days were filled with doing things for him and working. But now, who am I supposed to do things for?"

Marion offered a soft smile. "Yourself."

"I'm better when I'm with someone else. I often think about what Toby had wanted for me. He told me to date again, and I wouldn't hear of it, but he knew me better than I knew myself."

"Would you be up for dating someone else?" Marion asked.

"If you'd have asked me six months ago, I'd have said no, but I wonder, sometimes, if having someone in my life would open me up to my future instead of keeping me in this loop of grief."

"Let things unfold. You never know what could happen," Marion said. "And for now, until you find that perfect someone, I've got your back. And your pepper spray." She winked.

Heather took a warm sip of her coffee, the atmosphere of the coffee shop lifting her spirits. "How about you and Anthony? How are the two of you?"

"We're fine."

Heather frowned. "Fine or great?" When Marion shrugged, Heather added, "You know, we're waist-deep in my personal life. You're allowed to share yours."

"*Fine* is the best descriptor I've got at the moment." Marion blew a frustrated breath through her lips.

Heather leaned forward. "What's going on?"

Marion shook her head. "He and I are at an impasse. I want to start a family, but he isn't sure he wants one at all." She stared into the flickering fire as patrons chattered around them. "We had a pretty big blowup over it. I told him he should've mentioned that before we got married, and he snapped back and said, 'So you're saying you wouldn't have married me if you'd known?' I didn't have an answer." Her face fell, her eyes full of thoughts.

Having a family was something Heather and Toby had always talked about with excitement. And when he'd gotten sick, they'd cried together over the loss of their plans. She couldn't imagine the pressure Anthony's opposing view put on Marion.

Heather shifted in her chair to face her friend. "I'm sorry."

"I'd never asked him outright if he wanted kids, but when

I talked about the future I included family, and he didn't protest, so I'd assumed he'd want to start one. I feel like his silence was deception."

"Did he say why he never said anything?"

Marion shook her head.

"He didn't elaborate on why he doesn't want kids?"

Marion toyed with the breakfast in her lap. "He didn't have a great childhood. His dad could be a nightmare, and he wasn't very supportive of Anthony when he was growing up. I'm guessing it turned him off the idea of having kids."

"So, what are you going to do?"

"I truly don't know. I love him. But I don't know where to go from here. Scarlett has helped a little, but he always says, 'A cat isn't quite the same as bringing a child into the world. They don't talk back, and you can leave them alone without worrying.' He told me I can have all the cats I want, but he's right, that's not the same."

"I suppose, to use your wise words, 'Let things unfold. You never know what could happen.' Maybe he'll change his mind now he truly knows what you want."

"I hope so."

Chapter Five

After breakfast, they walked back to Bottle and Barrel. As they approached the door, Heather's phone rang. She checked the screen. "This number's called a few times now." She rolled her eyes, sure it was a journalist or someone similar.

"Answer it," Marion urged.

"If it were someone I knew, I'd have their name in my contacts."

It rang again.

"If they've called more than once, you might want to answer, given the Christmas card. Maybe it's someone calling to explain. Just hang up if it isn't."

Against her better judgment, Heather answered. "Hello?"

"Oh, hi..." said a man's voice. "I tried to call before about Toby's album and an award it's up for. My name is—"

"You're a reporter?" she cut him off. The vague memory of his voicemail came back immediately, and she tensed.

"Uh... not really."

"Well, I'm not doing any interviews."

"I wasn't asking for an interview. Are you planning on attending the country music awards in May?"

She didn't listen, focusing on Marion, who mimed, *Who is it?*

Heather offered Marion a flat expression, pulled the phone away from her mouth, and whispered, "Toby's up for an award." Then she turned her focus back to the caller. "I won't be attending."

Marion looked on, curious, clearly trying to make sense of the call with half the information.

"I'm not interested."

"I'd love to just have a few minutes of your time..."

"I said I'm not interested." Heather ended the call and dropped the phone into her handbag.

Marion tipped up her paper coffee cup and drank the last sip, then tossed it into a nearby trash can. "What would Toby say about all this attention?"

"Maybe that's why he suggested I get another bottle of wine," Heather teased. "Let's go inside."

The unique scents of oak, cedar, cinnamon, and cherry contrasted with the herbal fragrances of rosemary and thyme in The Bottle and Barrel. The whole place had a celebratory feel, with the floor-to-ceiling shelves lined with dark bottles and Christmas greenery. It was like stepping back into her memory, and she swallowed the small lump in her throat. If she closed her eyes, she was sure she'd feel Toby beside her. Was this his way of being close to her? Had he made good on his promise?

"May I help you?"

A woman with fashionably gray hair and a silk scarf dangling loosely around her neck walked toward them.

"I'm not sure," Heather answered, looking to Marion for what to do next, but Marion just stared at her, so she addressed the woman again. "My name is Heather Hart. I was told to come here." She fumbled around in her handbag and pulled out the envelope.

"Oh! How lovely." The woman gestured for them to follow, and she led them to the long dark-wood counter where she went around to the other side and retrieved a bottle of Tennessee blackberry wine. Around the neck was a red velvet ribbon and hanging off it another red-and-white envelope with a green wax seal. She held out the bottle. "This is for you."

Her heart pattering, Heather took it and inspected the label. It was *the* bottle of wine—the same brand she'd had that night with Toby.

"You're giving me this?"

"A young man has already paid. He asked if I'd tie the note to it."

"Did he tell you his name?" She could barely get the words out through her rising emotion.

The woman shook her head. "He didn't. When he bought it, he said it's a Christmas gift, and he specifically wanted this bottle. It had something to do with a special time you'd remember."

"Thank you," Heather said in almost a whisper.

"Of course. What a delightful idea for a Christmas surprise. He must love you very much."

Heather's breathing became shallow. *It couldn't be...*

"Merry Christmas."

Another customer asked the woman a question, pulling her away, leaving Heather and Marion standing in the middle of the shop, and Heather feeling as if she'd seen a ghost. She looked back down at the bottle, blinking away tears, absolutely confounded.

Marion linked arms with her, as if she could hold her up if she crumpled to the floor. "Let's open the envelope in the car, shall we?"

Heather was glad for Marion's hold on her. Her knees were knocking as she hugged the bottle, wishing with all her heart that it could actually be from Toby. While she knew there was no way, she hoped that, somehow, he'd been able to reach her. Who else would've known about this?

Once they got back to the car, Marion started the engine to get the heat going.

"What will be in *this* envelope?" Heather wondered aloud.

"There's only one way to find out."

With trembling hands, Heather untied the bow, the ribbon falling loose in her lap. She slid her finger under the wax seal of the envelope and pulled out the paper inside. Tears swelled. She blinked them away to read the message.

> Who needs a perfect Christmas movie moment when we have a lopsided tree, a muddy hill, and each other? I've left you something there. You know the place.

"Okay, this is getting freaky," she said through the lump in her throat, her heart pounding.

Marion wrinkled her nose. "I don't get it."

"It's another memory that no one knows. When we went to get our first Christmas tree, I said I wanted the kind of experience that we could only have in the movies." Her voice broke and she cleared her throat. "So we drove to a tree farm way out in the country, near the most adorable town, and went tree hunting. But everything went wrong."

She slipped into the memory as she told Marion the story.

❄

"We're going up there." Toby slung the saw over his shoulder and pointed to the hill lined with spruce trees. They'd paid the entrance fee, and any tree they wanted was theirs.

Heather zipped her coat up to her chin with a shiver. She'd hoped for snow today, but the weather was a bit too warm to make it happen. Not warm enough, however, to keep her from freezing to death. She'd finished a cup of cider half an hour ago, and the warmth it had given her was long gone. But at least tonight they'd have their first-ever tree as husband and wife.

They got to the top of the hill and found the most gorgeous tree right away. It was tall enough to have prominence under their high ceiling and full enough to take over the corner where she'd planned to put it.

"That's the one," she said excitedly.

Toby bent down and began to saw, back and forth, as the wind howled.

Heather hopped up and down to keep the blood moving in her ice-cold body.

After a while, Toby righted himself. "Uh... There's a problem." He pointed to the trunk.

The courtesy saw they'd been given when they'd paid the entry fee had supposedly been "more than enough" when Toby asked if it could do the job, it being smaller than he'd expected. The attendant had assured them that it was sufficient for every tree on the lot.

She bent down to take a look. The saw hadn't even made a dent. "I guess the guy didn't know what kind of tree we'd be looking for." She covered her mouth to stifle her giggle.

"It's a twenty-minute walk back to the main building. We're closer to our car than another saw," he said.

"Well, either we walk back and get another saw, or we find a smaller tree."

Then, the sky opened and a cold rain fell in buckets.

Heather squealed, flapping her arms, unsuccessfully shielding her head from the deluge.

"Let's get any tree this saw will cut!" Toby called.

He ran around trying different trunks until he finally found a wood that was soft enough to give way to the blade. As the rain poured around them, he worked until the tree cracked and toppled over. Then, with haste, he picked it up by the trunk, and they dragged it down the hill to where they'd parked. He ran the saw inside and didn't bother to challenge the attendant.

It took both of them to get the muddy tree on top of the car. Rain soaked the ground, and Heather's boots sank in the mud, making her slip.

Toby quickly strapped it down, and they scrambled inside the vehicle. Both of them burst out laughing between their shivers and chattering teeth.

Then, out of nowhere, Toby put his soaking wet, freezing hands on her face, drew her in, and kissed her. "It's going to be a perfect Christmas," he said.

❄

"That stupid tree curved to the left, and the ornaments kept sliding off it the whole Christmas season," she told Marion, wiping a runaway tear that slid down her cheek. "But it was ours." She stared at the note. "No one knows that story either."

"Could Toby have told someone?" Marion asked.

"I can't imagine a single instance where he would. Those memories were like little treasures to him, and he kept them all to himself."

"Where's the tree lot? The note says there's something there for you."

"It's on the edge of Leiper's Fork—about fifteen minutes away."

Marion put the car in gear. "Let's go."

They were quiet as Marion followed the navigation on her phone to get them to the tree farm. The whole way, Heather moved between utter shock that this was happening, to emotional instability whenever the memories came flooding back. She took long, deep breaths, trying to keep herself calm.

The snow had thinned, making it easy for Marion's little car to get down the winding roads. But Heather couldn't get the idea out of her head that she'd wanted snow that day she and Toby had come to the tree lot, and today, she'd gotten it. While she thought he could walk on water when he was alive, she doubted very seriously that he could manipulate the weather from heaven. But it had certainly crossed her mind, given what had happened so far that day.

Just as it had been the last time she'd been there, the tree lot's main building was at the base of the hill, with what seemed to be the same elderly bearded man in denim overalls and a thick coat underneath. Marion parked the car in a spot right out front, and they went up to the open window of the building where a few people were paying to go up the hill to find their tree.

"Make sure you have a sharp saw," she said to one as they walked by.

They looked her up and down, confused, but nodded politely.

Heather waved to the man in the overalls. "Hi. I'm Heather Hart." She held up the envelope. "You wouldn't, by chance, happen to have another one of these waiting for me, would you?"

"Ah, look at that! You showed up." He brushed his hands on his overalls and turned to the back counter, grabbing another red-and-white envelope. He held it out to her. "The guy just dropped this off for you."

She looked around. "Just? Is he still here?"

"That's him, there." The old man pointed toward the end of the parking lot at a white SUV. It pulled out, spinning gravel, and headed down the road.

Marion and Heather locked eyes.

"Thank you!" Heather said as she and Marion took off toward the car.

"Did you catch the license plate or the make of the SUV?" Marion said, fumbling her seat belt in her hurry.

"No, but we can probably catch up to him." Heather set the envelope in her lap and held it there with both hands.

Marion threw the car into gear and punched the gas. Her little Honda grunted as the engine tried to catch up. A man tying his tree to his car yelled at them to slow down, his voice trailing to nothing behind them as Marion sped toward the end of the lot, kicking up pebbles. Then she had to slam on her brakes to let a family cross. The father eyed her, irritated.

"Sorry," she said through her windshield.

The father frowned.

When the group had made it safely to the other side of the lot, Marion turned onto the main road. The pavement was clear—not a soul in front of them.

They continued driving, Heather craning her neck at every country road on either side. "Where'd he go?"

"I don't see him."

After a while, it was obvious the SUV must have turned off the road somewhere and they'd missed it. Marion finally slowed down.

Heather squinted through the windshield. "He drove like a maniac when he saw the man pointing him out. And he didn't seem to want us to catch up."

"I knew it. Stalker." Marion turned the car around and started back toward town.

Heather took another deep breath, trying to make the ordeal make sense. She looked down at the envelope in her lap. "Should I open this?"

"Uh, yeah," Marion said.

Inside, Heather found a printout of the email receipt for a plane ticket and a hotel confirmation, both in her legal name. The addressee's email and information had been cut off.

"What's that?" Marion's attention moved between the ticket notification and the road.

"I have a plane ticket to Greenville, South Carolina, and a two-night hotel stay at one of the swankiest hotels there."

Marion's eyes widened. "Aaaabsolutely no. No, no, no." She shook her head. "You are not going to a random location when there's an unmarked SUV involved. That's got warning written all over it."

"Except Greenville is where Toby and I spent our first wedding anniversary. I saw that hotel and said one day we'd come back and stay there."

"I don't care." Marion was still shaking her head. "This freak is using your emotions to get you alone in a hotel. You are *not* going to be on the evening news on my watch."

Heather looked in the envelope. "There's no note in this one."

Marion pursed her lips. "Even more reason to tear it up and throw it away. Really think about it, Heather. I'm seriously worried. Isn't it odd that the person leaving these letters doesn't want you to see him?

"You're probably right. Toby wouldn't have told anyone this stuff. There's no way," she said, although now she had more reservations about how exactly this person was getting these specific details about her life. Did she, in fact, have a stalker? "Sorry to have taken you on a wild goose chase."

"Ah, the biscuits and gravy were well worth it. But we should probably put in a police report once we get back."

As they drove home, Heather couldn't stop thinking about what might be behind the ticket in her hand. Why did he want her to go to Greenville? Even with all her questions, it was still as if Toby were there, planning her holiday like he always had. It would be reckless to go. But if Toby had a message for her from beyond the grave, wouldn't it be just as reckless if she ignored it?

Chapter Six

After locking all the bolts on her door, closing every curtain, and scouring her house for cameras, Heather spent all night thinking about the notes she'd received, trying to determine a motive. She'd fallen asleep still meditating on possible scenarios. And in the morning, she woke before the sun, and started contemplating them again.

She should probably call the police and at least bring the situation to their attention.

She got up and padded across the room, clicking on a lamp. A low, buttery warmth flooded through the gray light that filtered in through her gauzy curtains. She plucked the plane ticket notification off her dresser. Departure at 2 p.m. tomorrow. So the person setting this up knew she'd get the wine and then go immediately to the tree farm to follow the bread crumbs. Otherwise, the ticket would've been for later. She went to the window and, with one finger, barely pulled the curtains to see if anyone suspicious was out there. Was someone watching her?

The thing was, all the messages had to do with Toby and wonderful memories *she* had with him. They weren't about his fame or his music at all. The whole idea freaked her out. She collected the red-and-white envelopes and her new journal from her dresser and took a pen from her nightstand. Flopping on her bed, she opened to a clean page and wrote her next message to Toby.

Toby,

I miss you. Over the last few days, I've been inundated with memories of us—wonderful memories. You might know this already—who knows—but sitting on my kitchen counter right now is a bottle of the same Tennessee blackberry wine we got that Christmas. It was given to me after receiving notes referencing some pretty personal stories. I'm nervous. I know you wouldn't have divulged any of this to anyone, so it doesn't make sense. And as heartbreaking as it is to relive the memories, another part of me feels closer to you when I get them. Was this your doing? I'm supposed to go to Greenville, and I'm worried it isn't safe to do it, but everything in my body wants to go just in case I get another message from you. I know that's irrational thinking, but I miss you so much it hurts. What am I supposed to do?

She stared at the page, as if waiting for an answer from him, but nothing came.

No closer to understanding what was going on, she slipped the envelopes into the journal and closed it. She read over the email receipt for the plane ticket again. Someone had to have bought it, and the address was deliberately cut off. She grabbed her phone, searched the number for the airline, and tapped call. After a few minutes spent selecting options, and an incredible wait, an attendant finally answered.

"Hi there," Heather said. "I was gifted a plane ticket, and I'd like to know the name of the person who bought it for me."

"I'm sorry," the attendant said, "we can't disclose the purchaser's name or payment information, due to privacy regulations."

Heather slumped and chewed her lip, thinking. "Is there any way I can determine the purchaser on my end? Say, the ticket number?"

"No, again, I'm sorry. We're bound by strict policies that prevent us from sharing personal data, including the purchaser's details, even to the traveler themselves, unless under court order or for law enforcement purposes."

"Okay, thanks. Oh, and what personal information would this person have had to know to book my ticket?"

"They'd need your full legal name, date of birth, gender, email address, and phone number. I do apologize. I wish I could be of more help."

"No problem. Thanks."

"Happy holidays."

Heather hung up. If she called the authorities about this, perhaps they could figure out who'd bought the ticket. But if the ticket wasn't something sinister, they surely wouldn't find out who'd bought it in time for her to use it. Getting a detective to begin paperwork, her making a statement, and eventually the calls to the airlines could take days, and she didn't have that kind of time to figure out whether to go.

This person had to know her birthday, email address, and phone number. All of that was private information and under her legal name. How would this man have known that about her? Could a family member have given this information to someone? She decided to call her mom.

"Hi, honey," her mom said.

"Hey, Mom." Heather rolled over on the bed and stared at the ceiling.

"Whatcha doing?"

She told her mom what had happened since getting the first letter in the mail. "You or Dad haven't given any of my information to anyone, have you?"

"Goodness, no," her mom said. "With Toby in the spotlight like he was, we would never give anything to anyone. Could it be Marion or one of your other friends doing a nice surprise for you?"

Heather replayed the events in her head. "I don't think so. Marion doesn't lie very well, and she was pretty shocked. Also, there's the white SUV. I don't know anyone with a white SUV, and I've never seen one in connection with Marion."

"I don't want to throw caution to the wind, but it seems awfully kind to be something ominous," her mom said. "But you can't be too careful these days. Satan masquerades as an angel of light."

"Well, if you hear of anything, let me know."

"You aren't going to get on that plane, are you?" her mom asked.

"I'm not going to do anything that I think might put me in harm's way."

"Okay, hon. Call me if you need me."

With no other possible ideas, she got off the phone and got ready for the day. She hadn't checked her mailbox. Maybe there was another envelope that would give her more information. She slipped on her shoes, locked up her apartment, and headed down the hallway to the elevator.

In the lobby, a few people passed her. Heather studied their faces, paying attention to their movements to see if they were suspicious or not. When they got into the elevator she put the small key in the lockbox and turned it, opening the little door. She pulled out a few pieces of mail and flipped through them. The door to the lobby opened and a man walked in. She couldn't help but notice his dark hair and tall build. Could that have been who the mail lady had seen? He opened a mailbox, grabbed a fistful of mail, locked the door, and then hit the button for the elevator. When he stepped in, he made eye contact with Heather before the doors closed, giving her a shiver.

She hadn't realized, until now, how many strangers lived among her. She'd never thought about it before, but in such a large building, she didn't know half these people. Because of Toby, some of them knew who *she* was. Whenever he was with her, it was common for bystanders to steal glances at them or whisper among themselves.

Being in the public eye had never bothered her as much as it had Toby. Nashville residents were desensitized to seeing celebrities, and they generally left them alone. She didn't think twice about someone recognizing her, but now the act carried a different weight. It was as if they were all holding secrets about her, knowing her private memories, and digging into her personal information.

She hurried back to her apartment, quickly entering and locking the door behind her.

Her phone rang, and she jumped out of her skin. With everything being a potential lead, she answered it.

"Hello?"

"Hi. Don't hang up. I'm writing about Toby—"

Not this guy again. She cut him off. "Toby made it clear he didn't want the attention to be on anything but his music."

"Well, I'd like to also ask you about the awards..."

"He didn't go to awards shows, so I'm not either. I'm truly not interested in what you have to say."

"Hear me out."

Given what she was already dealing with, the last thing she needed was more of her personal life out in the open. "I'm sorry." She hung up and blocked the number, her whole body trembling. She considered calling the police and searched for the non-emergency number. Before hitting the call button, she paused, tears welling up. The wild swing of emotions was getting the better of her, and the last thing she wanted to do was be interrogated by police to get a handle on the story. Also, given Toby's fame, and how easily things could get leaked, did she want this drama out in the public? It could get splashed all over the magazines, and it would draw attention to her and her life. Maybe she shouldn't...

She'd stay in her apartment today and lay low.

Chapter Seven

"What have you been up to?" Marion asked Heather the next day.

"Nothing. Yesterday, the highlight was checking my mailbox downstairs, and, while drinking my new blackberry wine, I cleaned the apartment." She lay back on the bed.

What she hadn't told Marion was that she'd had the wine so she could spend the day buried in memories of her and Toby. She'd only cleaned in an effort to dig herself out of the past and force herself into the present. With the coded letters, she was afraid to go anywhere, but staying in their apartment alone sent her into a stupor of missing Toby and wishing their life could have turned out different somehow. Why did he have to go so soon?

"Any more Christmas envelopes?" Marion asked.

"No." She'd been both disappointed and elated by the fact that she hadn't found another letter, if that was possible. While she wanted nothing more than to hear from Toby, the reality of what those letters probably were was terrifying. She hadn't been out at all yesterday. She'd even cooked at home, and she never cooked.

"So, what are you up to today?"

"Big day already. I worked out in the house, showered, and even did a burnt-sienna hair-color treatment at home."

"Wow. What're you getting ready for?" Marion asked.

"I don't know."

She eyed the papers for the plane ticket and hotel stay sitting on her dresser. Despite worrying that someone might be stalking her, all morning she'd swung wildly between shutting herself up in the apartment forever and going to Greenville. Security was high at the airport, no one could bother her on the flight, and she could hire cars to get to and from places. Despite the possible risks, something pulled her toward going. Perhaps it was an irrational need to manage her grief, but whatever it was, the idea wouldn't let go of her.

"I could always fly to Greenville if I get bored," she said.

Marion laughed, evidently thinking Heather was joking. "I'd shy away from anything that might put me on the next episode of *Dateline*."

Heather rolled onto her back and pulled the pillow under her head. "Seriously. I keep asking myself what will happen if I don't show up."

"You maintain your freedom and safety?"

"What if I'm supposed to go? What if I miss something incredible?"

Marion groaned.

"What?"

A sigh came down the line. "There's no way you should go by yourself, and I can tell by the slight yearning in your voice that you're going to end up on that plane."

Heather sat up, excitement filling her. "Would you want to go?"

"I can't. Anthony's got a huge work party for his law firm this weekend that I have to attend. I'm trying to put forth some effort and embrace our couplehood."

Heather's shoulders fell. "I don't know what to make of these letters. But I also can't just ignore them. Whoever's behind this has put in some effort. At the very least, I need to try to figure out their motives."

"I don't like the idea of you going by yourself and staying in a hotel that the person who sent these things chose for you. If they do have malicious motives, you'll fall right into the trap."

"What if I stayed in a different hotel?"

"You're a regular Nancy Drew."

She grinned. "The only thing is, if I'm supposed to get something when I arrive, it will probably be in the hotel that was booked with the tickets."

"They could literally have their name on your room and have a key to it, Heather. I wouldn't stay there."

"I could stay there but get my own room under an alias."

Marion blew out a loud breath. "You make me so nervous."

"If this person wanted to hurt me, wouldn't they have met me at the first location and kidnapped me then? Instead, I got wine and then the tickets, and then, rather than trying to abduct me, the SUV took off in the *opposite* direction, literally running from me."

"True... So you're actually gonna go?" Marion asked.

"I think so."

"Please be careful. Call me as soon as you get there."

"Okay. It's a quick flight, and I'll call you the minute I land."

After a few more cautious warnings from Marion, Heather got off the phone and called the hotel, booking herself a room under the alias Missy Harland. With the email in hand, she checked in via the airline's website using the confirmation number from the email. Her boarding pass came through, and she put it in the digital wallet on her phone.

Her trip organized, she pulled her suitcase from the closet. Her mind went back to the last time she was in Greenville with Toby. She'd need a pair of comfortable sneakers suitable for walking. When they'd gone, she'd worn new boots, and Toby had had to carry her piggyback through Falls Park.

December would be cold. She packed with the expectation of crisp mornings and chilly afternoons. Into her suitcase went a warm coat, a few cozy sweaters, and long-sleeve tops she could layer easily as the weather shifted. She added jeans and a couple of pairs of leggings. The evenings could turn frigid, so she tucked in a scarf, gloves, and a knit hat, along with a lightweight rain jacket in case of winter showers. Finally, she added travel-sized toiletries, minimal makeup, and her charger.

In her backpack, she stowed some lip balm, hand sanitizer, a couple of novels for the flight, a big pair of sunglasses to help disguise who she was, and her new journal. She zipped up the bag, prepared for her winter getaway. Underneath the monotony of the tasks, there was an element of anticipation, despite the possible danger.

She stepped back and put her hands on her hips. Just like that, she was ready to go. But what would she be walking into? Why had she been given the ticket in the first place? What was the point of all this if not to make her feel as if Toby was with her?

"Are you somehow making this happen?" she called out to Toby in the middle of her empty apartment. As always, she was met with silence. "I guess I'll find out."

With one last look around her apartment to make sure everything was in order, she slipped on her backpack and, with ticket in hand, dragged her suitcase out the door.

About twenty-five minutes later, she was parked and at the Southwest Airlines bag-check kiosk, entering her information. The airport was swarming with holiday travelers.

She waited in line, unloaded her bags, pulled up her ticket, and headed over to the security checkpoint. Once through the massive line of passengers, she stopped to take in the glittering trees and merry music humming through the lofty expanse of Nashville's BNA airport. Families rushed to their planes, while others chatted happily at restaurant tables with red-and-green gift bags at their feet. There was a noticeable lift in the air with the holiday. She looked around to see if there was anyone suspicious lurking; however, she found nothing but fellow travelers.

Feeling jovial and a bit more relaxed after going through security, she went down to the coffee shop on the way to her plane and ordered a seasonal beverage, then found a seat among her fellow passengers, dropped her backpack at her feet, and called Marion.

"I made it to the gate, with a few minutes to spare," she said when her friend answered.

"That's good. No weirdos?"

"Already checked. None so far." She looked around again. "Mostly couples and families on this flight. There is a single person over by the window. He's got a magazine under his arm, a cup of coffee, and..." She squinted. "Maybe a laptop bag? He looks well put together."

"If he offers, *don't* drink the coffee. It could be laced with something."

"Why would I drink a random man's coffee?" Heather laughed, causing the woman next to her to glance over. "And I already have some. I got it on the way to my gate."

"Does he seem suspicious?" Marion asked.

Heather took in the slight gold in the man's dark-brown hair, the square of his clean-shaven chin, and his strong shoulders. He wore a pair of jeans, a sweater, and a tailored coat that buttoned up the front. "Not at all. He looks like he's on a business trip or something."

"Keep your wits about you. Call me when you get to the hotel."

"Okay."

She ended the call and slipped her phone into her bag. With time to spare, she dug around in her backpack and pulled out one of her novels, opening to the first chapter. It didn't take long before she was lost in the story, sipping her peppermint mocha, the bustle of holiday crowds fading into the distance.

Before long, it was time to line up to board the plane. She marked her place in the book, gathered her things, and got her ticket ready. Slowly, she shuffled forward, scanned her ticket, tossed her empty coffee cup into the trash can, and filed into the jetway. The airline attendant greeted her when she boarded, and she found her window seat without any issues.

"It's a full flight today, folks," the attendant said over the speaker. "There's not much room in the overhead bins, so please stow any excess baggage beneath the seat in front of you..." Heather pushed her backpack under the seat with her foot, slipped her book into the pocket containing the beverage menu and emergency exit instructions, and belted herself in. The two empty seats beside her would hopefully have a nice couple in them who would chat softly and let her out if she needed to use the restroom.

But after a few minutes, she realized she wasn't so lucky. A large man took the aisle seat, leaving the empty one between them for a stranger, who, given the size of the man, would be squished like a sardine between them. At least the flight to Greenville was only an hour and fifteen minutes, and while she'd had a full cup of coffee, she could probably hold it until they got to their destination.

People filed in, stopping to wedge their carry-ons into overhead bins and then making their way to the back of the plane. Then, the well-dressed guy with the magazine from the gate strode toward her. She hadn't noticed his green eyes until now. He stood out among the weary passengers with his crisp look and unbothered demeanor. When he caught her looking, she quickly turned to the seat in front of her and retrieved her book.

The man on the end of her row stood up, shuffling backward, and in slid Green Eyes, dropping down between them. She kept her focus on her book, but wasn't reading. He was jostling things, pushing his laptop bag under the seat and rearranging himself as he got settled, his arms moving precariously into her personal space because there was nowhere else for them to go. He bumped her.

"Sorry." He flashed a smile that would stop traffic.

"It's okay."

He wriggled some more and fastened his seat belt while she attempted to focus on her book.

As the flight attendant gave the safety instructions, the plane eased away from the gate and began its slow roll along the taxiway. To avoid following her peripheral vision to the man sitting beside her, Heather turned her focus to the ground crew's bright wands through the window as they directed the plane toward the runway.

As ground control cleared them to line up, Heather opened her book again. She began to read where she'd left off, the plane crawling once more. Moments later, they took their place in line for takeoff and she decided to wait to read until they were firmly in the air.

Green Eyes had his magazine open. He caught her looking again, and she quickly jerked back to her novel, sending her bookmark to the floor of the plane by the window. She nearly pulled a side muscle trying to retrieve it in such a small space, and when her fingers finally landed on it, her book slipped from her lap and fell on the other side of her feet. She righted herself as the man next to her bent over to get it.

"I'm Nicholas," he said, and then handed her the book.

Why was he introducing himself? She never introduced herself to fellow passengers on planes. But, then again, she didn't usually drop books on their feet either. Still. They were supposed to follow the unwritten rule of not infringing on what little personal space each of them had, unless nature called or there was an emergency, like dropping her book. He could've just kept to himself and let her sink into her thoughts. But he was providing first names—a definite no-no in her world. Was it his first time flying?

"I feel like the flight isn't as awkward if you know the person you're sitting next to." He held out his hand. "You can call me Nick."

His voice had a familiar cadence. No, maybe not familiar. Like an old friend. She shook his hand, Marion's questioning chatter floating into her mind: *Is he a stalker?* Although he seemed to be traveling alone, with his kind eyes and gentle smile, he didn't look anything like a stalker. And with him next to her, she felt safer. Surely if someone had bad intentions, they wouldn't proceed with this broad, fit man chatting to her.

"I'm Heather," she said.

His gaze roamed her face curiously. "Nice to meet you."

"Same."

There weren't many in life who'd responded to her the way he just had. His full attention was on her, as if something as simple as her name was the most important bit of information he'd get that day.

She slipped her bookmark into her novel. "This is odd, though, don't you think?" She waggled a finger between them.

Interest filled his face. "Why?"

"I don't usually talk to other passengers on planes," she said.

"Hm." That little humph came out as if she was the oddball. "I don't talk to everyone I sit next to. But when I do, I think plane conversations bring out the most authentic versions of ourselves."

"*What?*" She couldn't help herself. That comment made absolutely no sense to her. "How so?"

He shrugged, one shoulder lifting. "We're suspended in the air with complete strangers, no exit, no personal space, no expectations. There's something unique about that. In no other time in our lives do we face it."

Heather considered this, her fingers resting on the cover of her book.

His smile widened just a touch. "You can be any version of yourself you want for a couple of hours." He glanced at the novel in her lap, then back to her. "Or you can be more yourself than usual, because your actions won't follow you when you land. I'll disappear into the swarms of passengers, and you'll be on your way to wherever it is you're going."

She let out a quiet laugh. "And who do *you* usually become on planes?" she asked. "Someone else or your true self?"

Nick glanced above the rows in front of him in thought. Then he turned back to her. "Someone who talks to a woman he might not approach in any other circumstance."

Her cheeks warmed at that, though she wasn't sure why. "Should I feel special by that comment?"

He met her eyes, sincere. "I don't know. I was just being truthful."

The plane turned on the tarmac and then was cleared for departure. The engines roared and they began to move forward, the plane jerking slightly as it made its way down the runway. Instinctively, she reached for the armrest. Her fingers brushed his arm. Neither of them moved right away. Good grief. He probably thought she was flirting. Although their exchange had definitely ranked up there with her most unsettling plane interactions.

"Well," she said, clearing her throat as she pulled back her hand, "I guess temporary honesty doesn't hurt."

Nick smiled, and she quickly turned and reopened her book. But as the plane gained speed, she found herself rereading the same sentence twice, now highly aware of him beside her; of the strange, weightless feeling as the plane gathered speed, until the wheels lifted smoothly from the pavement, and they climbed into the open sky.

The ping of the seat-belt sign momentarily distracted her, and she looked up. It wasn't like her to initiate a longer conversation. She could just stare at her book for the next hour and fifteen minutes. As the plane leveled off, she tried to read, but struggled, her mind full with the strange sensation of having just chatted with Nick. She didn't get to talk to strangers that often. His interest was nice. She probably shouldn't ask him anything else. But he'd started the whole introductions thing, and now it seemed weird to just shut off for the rest of the flight.

She closed her book. "So were you visiting someone in Nashville?"

"I'm from Nashville, actually," he replied.

"Oh, me too."

"I live in East Nashville," he said.

She nodded. "Midtown."

He flashed that smile. "A hop, skip, and a jump then."

Was she telling him too much? Could he figure out where she lived? Marion would scold her with those questions, surely.

"So are you connecting in Greenville?" she asked.

"Uh, no. I'm going to Greenville for work."

The flight attendant interrupted. "Drink orders?"

"I'll have a water," Heather said.

"Coke." Nick turned back to her. "How about you?"

"I'm heading to Greenville as well."

"What brings you to South Carolina?" There was an indescribable care behind his words, and that attentiveness showed on his face once more, making her feel she could tell him anything. It was as if he was hanging on her answer.

"Um..." What should she tell him? "I'm on... vacation."

His brows pulled together in an adorable way. "By yourself?" He asked the question, but it was clear by the slowness of his words that he already knew the answer.

Her discernment pinged, Marion's stern finger waggling in her mind. He looked more amused than worried about her traveling alone, however, which she found charming. The sparkle in his eye made it difficult to focus. If that wasn't enough, the cascade of thoughts about how she hadn't considered a single person attractive in the last year flooded her. Not the guy two doors down or the new barista at The Steaming Quill—no one. The feeling was foreign and slightly uncomfortable, like an ill-fitting shirt.

"No... I'm meeting someone there," she lied.

He nodded. Was that skepticism in his pout? She was a terrible liar. He could probably sense her fib from a mile away. She'd better stop talking to him before she had to answer difficult questions like "What are you going to do for three days?" She had no idea.

"Well, I'll let you get back to your magazine," she said.

He smiled politely and began leafing through the pages.

With a steadying breath, she went back to her book. Marion would never allow her to live it down that the one person who seemed to be traveling alone on the flight had ended up sitting next to her. *Nick.* That name didn't sound like it belonged to a murderer or a stalker. She'd call an Uber when she landed, jump in before Nick even noticed she was gone from the crowd—just like he'd said. Then they'd probably never meet again. She just had to get through the next hour or so beside him.

Chapter Eight

They landed at Greenville-Spartanburg International Airport, taxied to the gate, and then came to a stop. She'd read through three chapters of her novel, added a small bottle of water to her bursting bladder, and avoided any further chatting with Nick.

When it was time for their row to exit, he stood up and let her go in front of him. "It was nice meeting you, Heather."

"Same."

She rushed off the plane and made a beeline for the ladies' room. When she'd finished, she fluffed her hair a little in the mirror, and swiped on some lip balm, then exited and followed the signs for baggage claim. The coast was clear. Maybe Nick would have already retrieved his bags by the time she got down there.

She walked slowly just in case, to give him more time to leave. She stopped off at one of the newsstands and lingered for quite a while, browsing the magazines and bestsellers, trying to stall. And, to her delight, when she finally arrived at the baggage carousel, only a few bags remained. Nick was nowhere to be found.

After pulling out the paper with her hotel booking from her backpack and ordering a car to pick her up, she called Marion.

"Landed safely. I'm just getting an Uber." Then she told her friend all about Nick.

"He was attractive and chatty?" Marion asked. "*That's* the kind of person you should probably be talking to. You two could've hit it off."

"Maybe he isn't single," she said. "And that's not why I'm here. I'm following Toby's trail right now. I'm not in any kind of headspace to entertain a date." The word sounded odd on her tongue. She didn't want a date anyway.

"Text me when you get into your room, so I know you've made it. Are you going to use an alias?"

"Yes. I'm Missy Harland. It's the safest option."

"Okay, Missy, keep me posted."

Heather ended the call and retrieved her bags.

The car pulled up right when she arrived at the pickup location. She peered around, and no one was there except a woman holding her phone, looking as if she, too, was waiting on her ride. Thank goodness. Heather got in and gave the driver the address. And they sped off.

The city seemed to glow brighter with each passing mile. Storefronts along the outskirts shimmered with holiday decorations, and the trees lining the streets were wrapped in strands of white lights. As the driver crested the hill approaching downtown, the twinkling canopy over Main Street came into view—thousands of tiny bulbs suspended like snowfall. Garland draped the lampposts, wreaths hung from shop doors, and the sidewalks were dotted with people strolling along the festive streets. Greenville looked less like a small Southern city and more like a warmly lit Christmas postcard —different from the fall, when she and Toby had visited. She instantly wished she could show him how wonderful it was during the holidays.

The car wound its way to the valet loop at the hotel. The stunningly massive lodge was perched on the side of a waterfall and draped in Christmas cheer. She got out and the driver took her suitcase from the trunk, handing it to her.

"Happy holidays," he said before getting back into his car.

Heather waved as he pulled away and then she entered the grand lobby. A four-sided stone fireplace draped in fresh Christmas greenery anchored the space. Travelers dressed in their holiday finest were drinking cocktails and lounging in oversized furniture that looked so comfortable next to the fire that she decided she could spend the whole three days right there. She walked past a bar with velvet stools, buzzing with people, to reach the hotel desk, where she checked in as Missy.

She leaned forward and said under her breath, "I have another room as Heather Matthews, but I'm going to stay in the room booked under my alias, Missy Harland." She handed over the confirmation page with Heather Matthews printed on it and then showed her the phone confirmation for her alias. "Please keep this confidential."

The woman nodded slowly. By the suspicion on her face, Heather felt she should give her some explanation. "My husband is Toby Hart," she whispered.

The woman inhaled sharply, an excited smile spreading across her face. "The singer?" she whispered.

Heather nodded and looked around, but it didn't seem as if anyone had noticed their exchange. "Yep. While *I'm* no one famous, using an alias is a precaution I take for safety. I don't want any crazies finding me." She made a face.

"Of course, Miss... Harland. Here's your room key. The elevators are just around the corner. And something was dropped off just a few minutes ago. We had it waiting for you." She reached under the desk and handed her a familiar red-and-white envelope.

Heather looked around, noticing a camera in the ceiling corner. Other than that, no one seemed to be looking. "Do you know who dropped it off?"

"I'm not sure. Could've been a courier."

Heather quickly slipped the envelope into her pocket. "Thank you."

With her key in hand, she got into the elevator and hit the button for her floor.

The doors opened to an empty hallway, thank goodness. She maneuvered her suitcase over the threshold of the elevator and walked down the carpeted hall, scanning the numbers for her room. As soon as she got in, not even noticing the stunning table and upholstered chairs, the inviting king-sized bed with a fluffy, crisp duvet, or the waterfall view out a pair of sliding doors, she dropped her bags and opened the envelope.

Heather,

Over the years, I threw myself into my creative journey and the causes I was passionate about, and you went right alongside me without ever complaining. My biggest fault was thinking I had more time to fit in everything else. I should've taken more time to find out what you wanted to do, and I should've let you get dressed up and taken you on more trips like this one, where we had no agenda, just wandering around, doing whatever we wanted. I know you loved this hotel when we saw it during our anniversary trip to Greenville. We were starving newlyweds then and couldn't afford to stay here; I should have spoiled you later.

Let me pamper you now... Enjoy the view. More to come.

While others could look up that she and Toby hadn't had a lot of money when they'd first met, only a very few knew about their trip to Greenville that first fall or that they hadn't taken many trips apart from those for his charity work.

She scanned the words again, stopping on the last line. *More to come?*

With her pulse racing, she called Marion to tell her about the note.

"What does that mean—more to come?" Heather asked, pulling back the curtain to take in the literal waterfall that ran next to her private balcony.

"This is spooky. It's like Toby's really there," Marion said.

"It doesn't make sense. Who would he have told this to? He wouldn't... He literally wouldn't," she said, completely baffled. "You know the great lengths he went to in order to keep our lives private. There's no way he would've told someone these intimate details." She let the curtain drop back into place and sat down on the bed. "I used to tell him he should celebrate his fame a little bit, and that it was okay to let people in, but he was adamant that his privacy was all he had to himself, and he'd never give it up."

"Please be careful," Marion said. "I'm still on the fence with whether this is a stalker situation or not."

"I know. I'll keep my head on a swivel." She stood up. "I just got in, so I'm gonna go and try to relax for a little bit."

"Call me later."

"Okay."

Leaving the envelope on the table in her room, Heather realized how hungry she was. She decided to check out the hotel restaurant. Dinner for one with a view of the Christmas lights outside might be nice. She went downstairs and made her way to the softly lit dining room. The hostess showed her to a table.

Through the window, a Christmas market buzzed with people, and a tall Christmas tree in bright lights illuminated the walkway as a snow machine sent snow onto a flock of giggling children. She picked up her menu and scanned the choices, but really, she was thinking about Toby. She'd like to think this was some kind of Christmas present he'd orchestrated just for her, and not some horrible trick by a prowler who had somehow found out about these precious moments in their life together.

The waiter came over, collected the second place setting, and brought her some water. In the spirit of celebration, and because Toby's note mentioned pampering herself, she ordered a decadent cocktail with rum, black tea, hibiscus, spiced citrus oleo, and cardamom. With her drink order in, she sat back amid the candlelight and surveyed the room. A couple toasted with their glasses of champagne and a group laughed while someone at their table talked animatedly.

The place was filling up, a small crowd forming at the hostess's station. It didn't take long before all the tables were occupied. Good thing she'd gotten there when she had.

She'd settled into the comfort of her surroundings until she caught sight of a single person across the room. In the chair opposite the figure was a familiar laptop bag. While pretending to peruse the dinner choices, through the dim light, she tried to make out the eyes. A waiter went over to his table, and when the man turned to speak, she dove behind her menu.

It was Nick from the plane.

Of course he'd be staying here.

Chapter Nine

With nowhere else to look, Heather turned to the hostess who was trying but failing to seat a couple, with all the tables full.

The waiter brought Heather's cocktail.

When he left her table, Nick was staring straight at her. He threw up a hand and gave her a little wave. She waved back.

Oh no. He was getting up and walking toward her. She straightened in her chair.

"What are the odds?" He grinned down at her. Then he looked around. "Table for one?"

"Yes," she replied.

"But weren't you meeting someone?"

Shoot.

"Oh, they couldn't make it," she said, heat rising up her neck.

"That's too bad." He frowned and then looked around. "It's busy. And people are waiting. I'd be happy to share a table and have dinner with you, so you don't have to eat by yourself."

What was she supposed to say? If she told him no, she'd look like a jerk on so many levels. "That's a good idea."

"Be right back."

Nick went to speak to the hostess. Then he returned to his spot, let his waiter know, and gathered his things, bringing them over. He dropped his laptop bag at his feet. As Nick took a seat with his glass of beer, the waiting couple thanked them on their way to the table he'd just vacated. Her waiter returned the second place setting and handed him a menu.

"What are you thinking about having?" Nick asked, scanning the choices, relaxed, as if sitting across from her wasn't the strangest thing in the world.

"I was thinking about the scallops," she replied. "How about you?"

He pursed his lips, still reading the options. "I'm not sure."

Having dinner with another man felt foreign. It was the first time she'd done so since Toby. She sipped her cocktail, hoping the rum would help her unwind. Between the letters and all the travel, she was wound up pretty tight. Marion's words came to mind: *That's the kind of person you should probably be talking to...*

But should she? She'd just boarded a plane in the hopes of connecting with Toby, and while that was a ridiculous proposition, her decision was an indication of where she was emotionally. She wasn't ready. Not to mention, she didn't know this guy from Adam.

Over her menu, she took in his unassuming pout, the tilt of his head, and his slight lean on the table. He appeared to be a decent person.

"The bison fillet sounds good," he said.

Just then, the waiter came to take their orders. She went first. While Nick told the man what he wanted for dinner, Heather took the opportunity to get a good look at him. He wasn't wearing any rings, so from the looks of it, he wasn't married. He seemed to be around her age, maybe a little older, probably mid-thirties. His response to the waiter was genuine and thoughtful. And he seemed to have absolutely no idea who she was, which was refreshing and gave her a sense of safety.

When the waiter left, she asked, "So, what line of work are you in?"

"Research. You?"

"I'm an elementary school librarian."

His eyebrows went up. "That's an honorable profession."

"And yours isn't?"

The corner of his mouth lifted, and he picked up his beer. "I'm not shaping the minds of innocent children, promoting lifelong learning, and enriching their curiosity."

"You do make it sound noble. But where would we be without research? What kind of research do you do?"

"Sociological, mostly. Basically, I translate data from consumer studies, surveys—things like that—into reports to help businesses understand their customers, forecast trends, and shape marketing strategies. I minored in sociology in college, so while theory and professional studies were what drew me in, sadly, once I got out in the real world... my days mostly consist of data and number crunching."

"I'll bet that's still interesting."

"Sometimes. But I spend most of my time on my laptop, so it's nice to talk to a real human being." He tipped his beer and took a swig.

The candle flickered between them, bringing out the gold flecks in his eyes. He was easy to talk to. And she couldn't help but consider the odds that he'd be next to her on the plane and then show up at her hotel. Back in Nashville, they lived about fifteen minutes apart, and here they were, four hundred miles from home, sitting across from one another.

Why? Had fate played a hand? Or was their meeting totally random?

He eyed her glass. "So you're a cocktail drinker?"

"Not really. I felt festive tonight. It's such a nice restaurant, I thought I'd treat myself. I usually choose wine."

He nodded. "If you're feeling the holiday spirit, and you've got time, we could always walk around the Christmas market outside after dinner." He nodded toward the stalls, filled with candles, local honey, and holiday wares that lined the grounds.

She could do with a little retail therapy. "That would be nice."

What was she doing taking this handsome man up on his offer? He was derailing her plans. She'd come to follow the letters, and here she was, veering off course. Was she supposed to be doing that? Would she miss something? But Nick had an indescribable appeal, and he had her interested. She couldn't put her finger on exactly what it was about him that could do that—it was everything.

"Have you always lived in Nashville?" she asked, taking another sip of her cocktail.

"Yeah. I grew up by the lake and moved into the city when I went to Belmont."

She perked up. "My..." She was going to say her husband went to Belmont, but thought better of it. If she said that, she'd surely have to explain everything. She was enjoying being herself and not Toby's widow. Not that she'd tell him anything personal anyway. "I think I knew someone who went to Belmont."

He smiled and took another drink of beer. "How about you?" he asked. "Are you from Nashville?"

"I'm originally from Florida, but I moved to Nashville when I went to Vandy, and I never left." She dared not mention that she'd met Toby at a bar the summer before her college graduation, when she'd originally planned to move back home, but he'd changed the trajectory of her life forever.

Nick held eye contact just a tick longer than normal, revealing his interest. "So you said you're meeting someone? What happened tonight? Mind if I ask?"

Great. Should she admit she's alone? He seemed like a perfect gentleman. But there was a tiny voice in the back of her mind that reminded her to be cautious. At the end of the day, she didn't know him. Then a completely irrational thought flashed through her mind: *What does it matter? If he murders me, I'll just be with Toby faster.*

"I lied," she heard herself say.

His head cocked to the side.

"I didn't want to admit that I'm here by myself."

Marion would kill her if he didn't.

He pursed his lips. "That's smart."

"I didn't know you, so I was being careful. And my best friend makes me feel like everyone is a murderer."

He laughed. "Well, hm. What can I tell you about me that will prove I'm no murderer?" He scrutinized his beer. "I have a rescue dog that I think is part poodle. Her name is Ophelia, and when I take too long to walk her, she puts her leash in her mouth, exits through the doggy door, and walks herself around the backyard."

A strange affection bubbled up at this revelation. "How long have you had her?"

"Six years. My friend owns a shelter, and she was going to be put down. I told him I'd find her a home or take her myself."

"She sounds adorable. You couldn't find her a home?"

"I never looked. The minute I put her in my car, she laid her head on my thigh. I had to peel her off me to get her into the crate for the drive home. And when I let her into the house, she wouldn't leave my side. I finally sat on the sofa, and she jumped in my lap and tucked her head under my chin. It was like she was thanking me for saving her. I adopted her that night."

Heather put her hand to her heart. "Oh, that's so sweet."

"It was as if she knew I was her person before I did." He pulled out his phone and opened a picture of the dog, showing it to her.

The photo showed the poodle mix sitting on a worn blanket on a sofa, light filtering in from a window and catching in the loose curls along its face. One ear drooped a little more than the other, and her dark eyes looked straight into the camera with a calm, searching expression, as if she were trying to understand who was on the other side of the lens. Her coat looked freshly brushed but imperfect, a soft mix of cream and gray that curled tighter around the ears and loosened along the body. Behind the dog, Nick's apartment appeared clean and carefully kept. A coffee table in front of the dog held nothing but a coaster and a closed book. The floors were bare and uncluttered, the surfaces clear. The space felt unmistakably like a bachelor's apartment—practical, restrained, and quietly intentional, with just enough comfort to show it was lived in and nothing extra to suggest any chaos—a lot like how he seemed.

"She's adorable."

"Thanks." He clicked off his phone and set it face down on the table.

The waiter returned and asked if they'd like a second drink. Given how relaxed Nick was making her already, she decided it was best she retain all her inhibitions. She ordered a mocktail. He got another beer.

"We haven't considered *my* safety in all this," he said when the waiter had left them alone once more.

"What?" she asked.

"*You* might be a murderer. The Midtown murderer—has a ring to it."

He was incredibly cute... *With those looks, I'll bet he knows how to woo the women.*

"Want to tell me something interesting about *you*?" he asked.

She hadn't considered it until now, but for the last year, apart from losing Toby, she didn't really have any defining characteristics to her life anymore. She worked, and Nick already knew that. And then she came home and tried not to fall apart. There were times when she could muddle through life, but those moments weren't anything special—cleaning the house, grocery shopping, getting coffee with Marion...

"Cat got your tongue?" he asked.

"I'm not that interesting," she replied. "I don't have an adorable dog like Ophelia or anything. I just work and come home." She was ruining a perfectly lovely moment by being boring. Marion would've kicked her under the table.

"Come on," he urged. "There has to be something interesting. Tell me why you're in Greenville."

She bit her lip. She was doomed any way she answered. Either she had to tell him about Toby and really bring him down tonight, or she'd have to say she was following anonymous notes from her deceased husband, which sounded ridiculous in her head, so she could only imagine what it would sound like to him. In fact, she was actively wondering why in the world she'd been so impulsive in going on this trip.

The lightness in his expression faded, and he sobered. "You don't have to tell me. I was just curious."

"I just decided to have some me-time." The half-truth was better than the reality. "Sorry. I wish I could do this better." She waggled a finger between them. "I'm not used to having someone's undivided attention. It's been a long time."

He gazed at her, something indecipherable passing over his face. "That's a tragedy."

Tragedy, indeed. If he only knew.

"You say you just work and come home. But you're here for me-time? That's a step in the right direction, I'd say. We need to give you a few stories to take home."

Why would someone as charismatic as Nick want to show her a nice time? Why did he care so much? "Why are you so invested?" she asked, honestly.

His eyebrows bounced as he formulated an answer.

"Sorry," Heather said. "That was a little direct. But I want to know. People don't usually come up to me and make conversation the way you did. It's a little unexpected, that's all."

"I've learned a lot from Ophelia. She just needed a few good experiences and her life changed. So did mine. I think we all could do with making memories no one can take from us. It might change our lives."

As they sat in candlelight between the glittering Christmas trees, Heather wondered who this wonderful surprise was that had fallen into her lap.

❄

"Marion, I'm in big trouble."

Back in her hotel room, Heather rehashed her dinner with Nick. "We went out to the Christmas markets afterward. I got some bubble bath made with local honey, and I bought a bag of homemade chocolates. And Nick wants to have coffee in the morning."

"Why do you think that's trouble?" Marion asked. "It sounds amazing."

"I guess I don't see what he sees in me."

"He sees the awesome person I see, obviously," Marion said.

Heather fluffed the crisp hotel pillow. "There has to be a catch. Maybe he courts women on every trip. This little share-a-table act could be his go-to move. Next thing I know, he'll have gone through my credit cards and bought himself a ticket to skip the country."

"You sound like me, now. You were always the optimistic one of the two of us."

"It's too perfect, too easy. And I'm not sure I'm ready. I worried all night that I'd nearly bored him to death."

"Maybe it's meant to be, whether you've planned for it or not. That's why it feels so easy."

Heather rolled across the bed and pulled one of her chocolates out of the bag on the nightstand—hazelnut. She popped it into her mouth, the deeply rich flavor exploding on her tongue. "Or it's my downfall."

"Look, definitely keep your wits about you. You don't know him, and you are alone. But give him the benefit of the doubt too. From what you've told me, he seems incredibly nice."

"I wish you were here." She felt unusually vulnerable without her sensible friend to guide her every step.

"Me too."

"How are you and Anthony?" she asked, wanting to get the conversation off her. "Any breakthroughs?"

"He's agreed to counseling. We're going to see if a third party can help us navigate our differences about having and not having a child—a disagreement that has no answer. I'm not optimistic, but I'm going through with the sessions."

"That's a start," Heather said.

"I guess so... Hey, have you gotten any more letters?"

"Not since the one I got when I arrived. I purposely asked

Nick to wait in the lobby while I went upstairs in the elevator, in the name of safety. But really, I wasn't sure if I'd have an envelope waiting at my door or anything."

"That's smart anyway," Marion said.

"Yeah. He makes me a little too comfortable. I have to remind myself that I don't know him as well as I feel like I do."

"Well, if he isn't a con man, it sounds like you've got the start of something wonderful."

"We'll see."

"Call me tomorrow."

"Okay."

Heather got off the phone, padded into the bathroom, and got ready for bed. When she'd finished, she went back into the room and sat at the small table and chairs. She opened her journal, the envelopes tucked into the back of it, and wrote to Toby.

> *Hey you. I've had a weird night. I met somebody who makes me feel special, but the guilt that comes along with it is hard to swallow. When you and I got married, I never thought I'd have to let anyone else in. I never wanted to. I know you said you'd be okay with it. You've always wanted nothing but the best for me. But that doesn't make letting my guard down any easier. I don't want to stay stuck in my grief forever, but how am I supposed to move on?*

She put down her pen and stared at the words until they blurred in front of her. With her final question to Toby going around in her head, she got up, checked the lock on her door, clicked off the light, and climbed into bed. The thing that had hit her the hardest tonight was that in her heartache, she'd gotten used to the monotony of her days. And tonight the speed of life had accelerated, and she'd scrambled to keep pace with it.

Chapter Ten

A knock at Heather's hotel door sent her heart pattering.

She was already full of nervous energy while getting ready to meet Nick downstairs. The front desk hadn't given him her room number or anything, had they? Surely they couldn't, for privacy purposes, but even if they could, she'd told the front desk that she was under a confidential alias anyway. So who could it be?

Another knock.

She walked to the door and peered through the peephole to find a bellman. She opened the door.

"Missy Harland?" he asked.

"Uh, yes?"

He held out a familiar red-and-white envelope.

"Thank you," she said, taking it.

He nodded. "Of course."

Heather shut the door, carried the envelope to the table, and ripped it open. She now looked forward to these little surprises. *This* was why she was really here—she had to keep that in the front of her mind. Would she know when she'd received the last one? Could this be it? She didn't want to think about it. She read the note.

I have a question for you today: Have you had hot apple cider recently? If not, you should have a cup. So should everyone, right? Go to Windy Rock Orchard and get yourself one. Once you do that, you'll get the next message.

What? Drink apple cider? Why should everyone drink it?

She checked the time. Oh gosh. Nick was waiting. With a deep breath, she pulled herself out of her old life and lurched into the present one. With a quick check in the mirror, she darted out the door.

In the elevator, she sifted through old memories, trying to make sense of the message. Then it hit her. She and Toby did have apple cider in Greenville. Where had they been when they'd had it? A restaurant? Where *were* they? They didn't visit the orchard. They'd run out of time. There was nothing memorable about the cider, apart from the two of them simply being together. What was the point of his message? At least with the wine, she had a bottle to take home and a big memory to hold onto. But the cider—she wasn't getting it.

She walked through the lobby, past the bar and the flickering stone fireplace. On the other side of the hotel, in the restaurant, Nick, clean-shaven and freshly groomed, waved from an empty table. She went to join him.

"Good morning," he said, his face bright and well rested.

"Morning." She took a seat across from him.

A waiter appeared. "Welcome. Will we be having a

beverage this morning? We have fresh fruit juices, lattes, cappuccinos… We have French press, hot tea…"

Nick nodded for her to order first.

"A latte sounds wonderful. Do you have something sweet to put in it? Maybe honey or something?"

"We have honey."

"Perfect."

Nick ordered a black coffee.

The waiter left, and Nick leaned his forearm on the table. "So, what's on the agenda today?"

"I'm actually going to Windy Rock Orchard. I have a hankering for apple cider."

His green eyes sparkled, and it occurred to her that she should at least offer for him to go with her since they were both traveling by themselves. He'd surely decline, since he was there for work, and she could go about receiving the next letter.

"Would you like to come with me, or do you have to work?"

"Well, I do have to work on my research, but everyone should get to take a break sometime."

A mixture of fear and excitement overtook her, both pulling in different directions. While she enjoyed spending time with Nick, how would she explain the next letter if she got it at the orchard? She smiled. "You sure I'm not pulling you away from work too much? I know you hadn't planned on this today."

"I keep my own hours, so I can make them up when I get back to the room tonight."

"What are you researching at the moment?" she asked.

He wrinkled his nose. "I have to follow protocol and not disclose it. That's the rule."

"Oh," she said, impressed. "Are you working with a government agency or something?"

He grinned, sending her heart aflutter.

It had been a long time since someone had looked at her that way. The night before, when he'd given her an answer that stunted the conversation, she'd withered into silence, but this morning, her response came naturally, and it had made him laugh, which lifted her spirits more than anything had in a long time.

"Definitely not anything that intense," he said. "To be vague, this one mostly covers things like communication patterns and stability predictions, but it's been nice—not so many numbers. I'm meeting with a colleague here in Greenville. He's showing me the finished product before we present it to our client. It's been a long time coming, and we're really excited to have nearly made it to the end."

She'd been so caught up in her little world that it was nice to hear there were people like Nick going about their lives and making a difference. "It sounds so interesting."

He chuckled. "Eventually, the report will be public knowledge, and I'll be able to share it with you. Then you can tell me what you really think." He paused. "If we keep in touch. Will we?"

She hadn't considered what would happen after these few days. "Maybe," she said, oddly hopeful they would.

As easy as Nick was to talk to, he probably had tons of friends and a buzzing social life, which was quite different from her quiet, solitary life. Would she be able to keep up? Or would she weigh him down? And would they be hounded by the press if anything came of this? She could see the headlines now: "Toby's Widow Finds a New Beau." Was he ready for all that? She certainly wasn't sure if she would be. Should she warn him about it, come clean, before he got too invested? *It's still early*, she decided. She could wait and see what would happen after this trip.

The waiter returned with their coffees. He folded his arms behind his back. "Will we be having breakfast?"

"I'm hungry," Nick said. "How about you? My treat, if you want something."

"Oh, you don't have to..."

"I know I don't." He gestured toward her menu. "What do you feel like this morning?"

She scanned the choices quickly. "Just some eggs and toast, please."

"And you, sir?"

"I'll get the lobster omelet." Nick set his menu on the table.

Lobster omelet? Their orders explained the two of them perfectly. He was very much a lobster omelet, with all its interesting flavors and textures, while she was plain old eggs and toast.

When the waiter had collected their menus and left, Nick picked up his coffee. "I have to run out for that meeting, but I should be done with work around noon. We could grab some lunch somewhere and then go to the orchard if that works with your schedule."

Another meal together? They weren't even done with breakfast and they were planning lunch? But she couldn't deny the slight rise in her spirits at the idea of it.

"I mean, don't feel pressured," he added, when she hadn't responded. "I know you're here for some alone time. I just enjoy your company."

"No, no. It's fine. Why don't we meet in the lobby at twelve thirty?" she asked.

"I'd love that."

Chapter Eleven

"That would be three meals in a row with Nick since we got here," Heather told Marion on the phone once she'd gotten to her room. "That's strange, right?"

"Yeah. But it doesn't mean he's not a great person."

"He's definitely an extrovert, and he said he enjoys the company." Heather sat at the table, fiddling with the envelope edges hanging out of her journal.

"Ask him questions about himself. He doesn't seem to mind you doing it. Maybe once you get to know him, you'll feel more comfortable."

"The only problem is when I do that, he wants to know about me. I'm not ready to tell him about Toby. It'll drag us into all that—and it's a lot for someone who's just trying to kill time on a work trip."

"Given how things have lined up so far, he might surprise you. And if it is too much, you'll fly home and probably never run into him again."

Heather rubbed her forehead. "It's all a bit overwhelming. Why would he be so interested?"

"Because you're beautiful and kind."

"Thank you." Marion's words hit Heather hard. It had been a long time since she'd felt attractive. She'd better change topic before Marion had her tearing up. "So. Enough about me and my drama. What have you been up to today?"

"I have to go to the in-laws' tomorrow, so I've been baking cookies. I got last pick of the dishes to bring, and it was either that or a main dish. I was hoping to get a bag of chips or a couple bottles of soda..."

"Did you make those peppermint cookies you're so good at? They were a hit at the staff luncheon."

"Of course I did. I have to keep up with Anthony's sister. She's always coming in with a tray of food that looks like it fell off a Pinterest board."

Heather laughed. "I wish I was there to help."

"Me too. You're the cleanest of the two of us, and my kitchen looks like a flour bomb went off in it. Scarlett keeps walking through the chaos and dragging it all over the house."

"You make me want to be there to cuddle that sweet little ball of fur."

"She's a mess. Literally."

Heather chatted a while longer and then got off the phone. Marion grounded her, tethering her to who she was, with a lighthearted worldview and without the constant reminder of her grief, which she needed right now.

She had to meet Nick soon, and after talking to Marion, she was wrestling with whether she should. She struggled to imagine moving forward in any capacity with someone when grief still clung to her thoughts. She weighed the comfort of isolation against the frightening vulnerability of connection. Did moving on mean letting go or simply learning how to carry her loss alongside unfamiliar possibilities?

But it's not as if I'm fully moving on—it's only a third meal.

However, accepting meant that she was taking the next step toward moving on. Was she ready to do that?

Still trying to make sense of the whole thing, she got up, went over to the sliding glass doors, and opened the curtains. Through the glass, the waterfall cascaded down the rocky surface, and beyond it was the view of the park. Across the expanse, joggers bundled in their winter wear made their way down the trails. Had Toby given her this gift? Was it possible? And if he'd somehow miraculously made it happen, was she being disrespectful to his memory by running around with Nick?

What was her purpose in all this? What was the big crescendo she was striving for? Was there one, or did everyone simply exist?

Leaving the curtains open to allow the muted daylight to filter into her room, she returned to the table and opened her journal. She needed Toby right now. He'd always been her confidant.

She flipped to a new page.

Hey you. I know you'd want me to move on and have a good life. We even talked about it, when I'd let you. I might have accidentally met someone. He seems thoughtful and genuine. I'm actually happy when I see him. The feeling surprises me, though, and in a sense, makes me a little uncomfortable. It's as if my future is pulling me forward, when a part of me—the reason I'm here in the first place—wants to remain in the past for a little while longer. If I could choose, I'd be the old me, with you. But I don't get that choice. I guess I have to keep going, changing. I wish you could somehow tell me that it's all going to be okay.

Maybe change itself was the crescendo she was looking for. Toby's absence followed her everywhere, a constant weight that reshaped her routines. She found herself grieving not only what she'd lost, but the person she'd been before the cancer happened, realizing that her life would never return to its previous shape. Processing the loss meant accepting the change it demanded of her. While Marion and her other friends helped her mask the grief with laughter and a change of subject, Nick seemed to force her to accept it. Because by feeling something when she was with him, she had to acknowledge that her time with Toby was fully over. Maybe that was why she was struggling to meet him right now.

She stared at the words she'd written to Toby, wishing he could talk back. His voice filtered into her mind. *Sheesh. You're already getting physical notes from me. What more do you want, actual miracles now?* She smiled.

Speaking of notes, he'd promised her the next one if she got herself a cider. So much for blowing off her lunch date. She'd better go if she wanted the next message. She checked herself in the mirror, grabbed her room key and her phone, and headed out the door.

Nick was waiting at the lobby bar when she came down.

"Getting an early start?" She eyed his empty glass.

A smirk surfaced. "Soda." After dropping some cash on the counter, Nick thanked the bartender and hopped off the stool. "After you." He gestured toward the exit.

A bellman opened the door for them, the cold winter air wrapping around her and giving her a shiver.

"The hotel restaurant is getting a bit claustrophobic, so I took the liberty of searching for something different. I called us a car. It should be pulling up," Nick said, leading her to the main drive.

So much for getting her own car to be safe...

"Where should we go for lunch?" she asked.

"Do you like pizza?"

"I do."

"Good. Because I also made the executive decision to get us a reservation in town. The ratings are great, and it's on the way."

Out of nowhere, a lump formed in her throat just as the car pulled up. Thank goodness for the distraction. Why was she so emotional? Nick opened her door and she climbed in, desperately searching for an answer.

As he chatted with the driver, she realized the pizza restaurant was what had done it. Toby had always taken care of the plans. He was great at it. All she'd had to do was show up. But since he'd passed, the weight of preparation had fallen on her shoulders, and only now did she realize how something so simple as making sure things happened on time had weighed on her. Because of it, many times, she'd opted to stay at home rather than try to find someone to meet her. In this one moment, Nick had illuminated how alone she'd been.

Luckily, by the time the car pulled away, she'd pulled herself together. Then, her phone rang.

"Do you need to get that?" he asked.

No one would be calling her. It was probably a reporter. She shook her head and silenced her phone. "I don't recognize the number. I'll just see if they leave a message." Turning her phone face down in her lap, she asked, "How was your meeting?"

"It was very productive. Everything looked amazing. I'm excited to show it to the client."

"When do you do that?"

"We've still got a little while. But my work on it is finished."

She checked her phone and whoever called had left a message. With all the strange notes she'd gotten, should she listen to it? After all, she was on her way to get cider. Had Toby managed to leave a voice message for her? Wouldn't that be incredible?

"You can listen to that if you need to." Nick nodded toward her phone.

"Okay, thanks." Awkwardly, she hit play and put the phone to her ear.

"Hello, Mrs. Hart, my name is Alex Branson from *People's Entertainment*. We were hoping to catch up with you to ask some questions about your late husb—"

Heather hung up. She tried to discreetly block the number, the way she had for all the rest, but Nick was watching her, so she didn't.

"Everything all right?" he asked.

"Sales call." She huffed out an unconvincing laugh.

Nick's attention lingered on her phone a tick longer than it should have.

She was going to have to come out and tell him about Toby. Maybe she would at lunch, or when she got the next letter. But should she? Would Toby want her to divulge their private affairs? He didn't even let her listen to his demos when he'd written a new song, so she felt nervous about telling Nick anything for fear that she wouldn't be honoring Toby. And once Nick knew who she was, he might look at her differently. She wanted to get to know him a bit more first.

The car stopped and let them out.

"What do I owe you for the ride?" she asked.

Nick shrugged her off. "Don't worry about it. It's easier if I just pay."

The restaurant occupied a narrow corner of one of the

city's historic districts, its tall windows glowing warmly against the dark stone of the building, trimmed with garlands of fresh pine and oversized red velvet ribbons. Inside, a towering Christmas tree stood near the bar, with understated gold ornaments and trimming that echoed the marble-topped tables and dark-wood chairs.

Nick held the door open for her. The air carried the rich fragrances of garlic, truffle oil, and fresh basil.

Nick gave his name to the hostess, who took them past the open kitchen, where chefs in crisp white coats worked at a stainless-steel counter in front of wood-fired ovens. One of them slid a pizza onto the silver pass, where the waiters retrieved it. It steamed, arranged with a sprig of basil and rosemary like carefully composed art—charred at the edges, lavishly topped with various meats and vegetables. The waitstaff hustled around amid the quiet warmth of the holiday season.

Nick pulled out her chair, and she took a seat. He was a perfect gentleman. He'd been in the lobby waiting for her, he'd planned lunch, and he'd taken care of the ride over. She hadn't done a thing to deserve his attention. She'd been quiet, not forthcoming—skittish, really. Yet he never offered anything other than genuine kindness. She should stop tiptoeing around and get to know him more.

Once they were settled, before her nerves got the better of her, Heather dove right in. "You never told me your last name. What is it?"

He placed his cloth napkin in his lap as a waiter filled their glasses with water. "Monroe."

The man took their drink orders. They both got a soda.

When they were alone again, Nick picked up his menu. "What looks good to you?"

She suddenly worried that she'd overstepped, even though she'd only asked his last name. But once she knew that, she could find him and vice versa. "You don't want to know *my* last name?"

He peered over his menu. "I figured you'd offer it if you wanted to tell me." He set down his menu and made eye contact. "At dinner last night, you didn't seem super excited to talk about yourself, so I figured you were a private person."

"It's Hart," she said. "Heather Hart." She mentally braced herself for the recognition that happened whenever she gave Toby's last name.

He gazed at her, a small smile playing at the edges of his lips. She'd made him happy by sharing something so basic. And, to her delight, he didn't show any signs of knowing who she was. If he wasn't terribly versed in Toby's personal life, which from all accounts he probably wasn't, he wouldn't know that Toby had a wife named Heather. So the connection had been lost on him. Perfect.

"What were you like as a kid?" she asked.

His grin widened. "You're talkative today."

"If I'm going to have a third meal with someone, I want to get to know who I'm eating with. One meal is a fluke. The second, a product of good timing. But the third... That changes things."

He lit up with interest.

"So, what were you like as a child?"

"As a kid, I talked a lot."

She laughed. "I could see that."

"I grew up at Old Hickory Lake, though, which taught me how to pause and listen, how to notice when someone needed quiet instead of noise." He sobered, some unknown thought coming to him. "I learned that even the smallest splash I made in that water could reach farther than expected. I never tossed a stone without considering how far the ripples would travel."

"Are you talking about the lake or something else?" she asked.

His gaze met hers, an undisclosed answer hanging on his lips, as if he wanted to tell her a deep, dark secret.

Two sodas appeared in front of them. "Are you all ready to order?"

The question tore through the conversation, and they both rushed to find a suitable option in their menus.

"I'll do the spinach and feta personal-sized pizza," she said, choosing the first thing she landed on.

"That sounds delicious," Nick agreed. "I'll have the same."

"I'll get those in for you."

The waiter left, and she could feel them both scrambling to regain the moment.

"How about you?" Nick asked. "What were you like when you were young?"

So whatever was on his mind, he was effectively avoiding? But she could understand. Perhaps there was something in his past he didn't want to bring up. And, fair enough, given they'd only just met. In a way, both of them having unsaid pasts strengthened the bond she was building with him.

"I was quiet mostly. I read every free moment I got," she finally said.

He nodded, his gaze swallowing her. "It's pretty obvious you have a lot of thoughts in that head of yours that don't make it out of your mouth."

"You can see that?"

"Yes."

"Maybe one day, I'll tell you some of them."

He brightened. "One day? As in, we'll still be talking in the future?"

Happiness fluttered through her. "You never know."

Chapter Twelve

After a long, meandering drive on the fringes of the city, they pulled up at Windy Rock Orchard.

"Let me know how much I owe you for the trip," she said as the car drove away.

"I got it."

"You got lunch as well," she noted. "And the ride to the restaurant."

"I don't mind. It's nice having a travel companion. I wouldn't have done any of these things if you hadn't come with me. I'd have been holed up in my hotel room, tapping away on my computer."

"I'm infringing on your work time," she worried again.

"I was mostly here this weekend for the meeting. I can manage."

The orchard hummed quietly but steadily with visitors. Nick and Heather walked the long path past the ordered rows of apple trees, their branches bare and dark against the pale sky, lightly dusted with frost. Workers moved between them in heavy coats and gloves, pruning limbs, shaping the trees for spring.

They meandered through public conversational areas of metal firepits encircled by rustic chairs, while tractors crunched slowly along dirt paths, hauling stacks of cut branches down the aisles between the trees. Even without leaves or fruit, the orchard felt alive—resting, preparing, and quietly at work beneath the frozen ground.

The cozy atmosphere, the scents of spiced apple and burning wood, and the crisp chill in the air made walking next to Nick feel like a date, as if she wanted to find a chair next to a fire and snuggle into his coat.

When they'd made it into the barn, the heat hit her, giving her a residual shiver as it pushed the cold out of her body. What, on the outside, had appeared to be an unassuming, red-painted clapboard barn was transformed into an upscale eatery with light fare. The tables had red-and-white gingham tablecloths, there was a stone fireplace with a roaring fire, and shelves of handcrafted jams, apple butters, wines, and pies. A Christmas tree, decked out in rustic plaid bows and white lights, glittered in the corner, and a mismatched row of knitted stockings hung from the fireplace.

Heather and Nick walked up to the counter at the back. A woman in a flannel coat, fingerless knitted gloves, and a well-worn pair of jeans shifted and stacked crates while others tended cider barrels along the wall.

"Hey, y'all." She brushed her fingers on her thighs. "Welcome in."

"Thank you," Heather said, peering up at the menu. "I'll have a cup of your apple cider." She looked over at Nick. "I'll get this. What do you feel like?"

"I'll have a cup as well."

"Two apple ciders. Anything else?" the woman asked, punching keys on the register.

"That'll be it." Heather could have given her name and

asked if there was a note waiting for her, but she chickened out with Nick standing there.

She swore the woman stared at her for a tick longer than she should have and then nodded. "I'll bring them out to ya."

With a feeble smile, Heather paid for the drinks, and then she and Nick settled at a table for two next to the fire.

Being with Nick was becoming oddly comfortable, which made no sense given she'd only just met him. Perhaps it was his unassuming, relaxed demeanor, the way nothing seemed to ruffle his feathers. He seemed genuinely happy to sit with her in the middle of an apple orchard, when he'd had no plans to do so prior to meeting her. He'd paid for meals, accommodated her, and seemed sincerely interested. She kept waiting for the other shoe to drop.

"Deep in thought again?" he asked.

"I was just wondering why you agreed to do all this with some random person you met on a plane."

His features shifted, a serious expression emerging. "I surprised *myself*, actually. I don't know. You're easy to talk to, and I find it strangely intriguing figuring you out."

Marion's voice filtered in: *Maybe it's meant to be, whether you've planned for it or not. That's why it feels so easy.*

The woman from the counter brought them each an oversized mug, full to the brim with steaming, spiced cider, adorned with a cinnamon stick and a peppermint drop on the saucer. Had she lingered before she left, or was Heather being paranoid? It was busy enough that, if the woman was waiting to give something to her, she probably couldn't guess that Heather was looking at her.

Nick held up his cider. "To happy surprises," he said.

With two hands, she clinked her mug against his and took a sip. The cider tasted honeyed and decadent, with gentle notes of cinnamon and spice against a soft tartness of apple, which balanced the sweetness.

But once the rich flavor had settled on her tongue, a different sensation took over. This one not quite as pleasant. She set down her mug and eyed the woman at the counter, considering whether one of Toby's notes might be lying behind it. Had the woman wondered if the note was meant for Heather, or had the woman's reaction to her order and then again at their table all been in Heather's mind? Nick had become a distraction—albeit a handsome one—but she was meant to get another note. Toby had said so, hadn't he?

"Are you thinking about having the pie as much as I am?" Nick asked, dragging her from her thoughts.

"Hm?"

"You keep looking over at the counter. Are you eyeing the apple pie? It would be a nice dessert, wouldn't it?"

"Oh," she said, relieved he'd fabricated an answer for her. "I was considering it, but I'm pretty full after the pizza."

He leaned forward and squinted at her. "Something's on your mind. I won't pry, but I'm here if you want to tell me anything."

She deliberated. *You don't even know yourself what's going on.*

"Thanks," she said. "I'm really fine. So tell me, when are you flying home?"

"It's a quick trip. I leave tomorrow."

"Oh! I leave tomorrow too. What time is your flight?"

He pulled out his phone and pulled up his e-ticket. "Eleven."

She laughed. "I'm probably on that flight."

That now-familiar interest flickered. "Then back to reality," he said, with unspoken thoughts lingering in his gaze.

"Yes."

What were the odds that they'd be leaving the same day and possibly on the same flight? It was as if God, Himself, were moving her life along, whether she wanted Him to or not, forcing her hand. If they flew home together, they'd have another couple of hours and then they'd both be in Nashville. If that happened, it would give her time to gather enough courage if she decided to tell him everything right before they landed. But how much, if any of it, would Toby have wanted her to divulge? She hadn't been in the habit of dishing out her life story to people before, so why start now? She didn't have anything to hide, but all she could think about was Toby looking down on her and seeing her going against his wishes. It was enough to paralyze her.

"We should share a car to the airport," he suggested, as if reading her mind.

"Yes. Let's."

She'd only been gone two days, and she already had a different outlook, thanks to Nick. Meeting him had pulled her from her rut and changed her in ways she could never have expected. The difference was unreal.

"Could I see you again when we get home?" he asked.

Exhilaration coursed through her. "I'd love that."

They continued chatting about the cider, the fireplace, how nice it was to be able to sit together in such a festive environment.

Ten minutes went by. Then twenty. The woman from the counter had passed their table twice, and there'd been no sign of another note, so Heather seemed to be in the clear, thank goodness. While Heather didn't want to have to explain herself, she was also quietly trying to figure out how to ask the woman if there was a note before they had to get up. It was getting crowded, and people were looking for places to sit. How long could they stay there?

"Hey, I want to get you a slice of apple pie to say thank you," she said. "And my food has settled. It sounds divine."

He pushed away from the table. "I'll get it."

"No, no!" She stood up and grabbed his arm. "I've got it. You save our table."

"Okay." He looked at her questioningly.

She offered a little wave of her fingers. "Be right back."

After waiting in line for a few minutes, she got to the woman. "Hi." She peered back through the crowd at Nick. He was checking his phone. With a deep breath, she returned her focus to the woman. "I'm *Heather Hart*."

The woman offered an awkward smile, her eyebrows rising in mock recognition.

Heather glanced over her shoulder again. Nick was still scrolling his phone.

"Do you have an envelope or a note for me?"

The woman frowned, clearly puzzled. "Should I?"

"Yes, I thought someone might have left it for me. It's red and white, with a green wax seal."

The woman looked under the counter, moving papers and boxes. "I don't see anything. Who left it for you?"

"Uh, I'm not sure. It should have my name on the outside."

"Let me ask in the back." The woman jogged over to a swinging door and disappeared.

Customers in the line behind her were getting restless. When she checked on Nick, he'd looked up from his phone. She offered a nothing-going-on-out-of-the-ordinary smile.

The woman returned. "Nope, it doesn't look like anyone left something here."

"That's okay," she said, slightly baffled. Toby's note had just said once she got cider, he'd give her the next message. He hadn't said where. The good news was that, with no possible note coming her way, she could relax and enjoy her dessert with Nick. "Could I just get two slices of apple pie?"

"Yes, ma'am."

She paid for them and went back to their table.

"Everything go okay?" he asked.

"Yeah. She just had to check in the back to see how many pies were left."

His expression pinched with confusion, and he eyed a stack of about fifty pies on a nearby table.

She followed his gaze. "I think they have certain ones for sale and others for dining." Her stomach churned. She was uneasy lying to him. Even if her untruth didn't impact his life in any way, he'd been so honest with her that she felt awful. She decided that if she ever told him about Toby, she'd come clean on this little fib. He'd forgive her, right?

To her relief, someone from the kitchen brought over their plates of pie. The slices sat steaming on the plates, the flaky crust slightly cracked from the heat. Thick chunks of apple glistened beneath the lattice top, and wisps of warmth rose into the air, carrying the sweet smell of baked fruit and butter. With the crackling fire, Nick next to her, and Christmas music floating over the crowd, it was one of those holiday moments she'd want to tuck away for safekeeping on a lonely night.

"This looks incredible," Nick said, pressing his fork through the point of the slice. "In all the times I've been to this city, I've never come here. Thank you for the opportunity. I wouldn't have come without you."

His kindness warmed her. "I'm glad we could both come."

She might not have gotten an old memory while she was here, but she couldn't shake the idea that she might very well be making a new one. What was happening?

Chapter Thirteen

Full of festive excitement, Heather said goodbye to Nick in the hotel lobby and got into the elevator. She'd had a great day. She couldn't wait to get back to the room and call Marion to tell her all about it.

The doors opened onto her floor, and she stepped out, making her way to her room. When she got to her door, she gasped. Leaning against it was another envelope. She snatched it up and rushed to let herself into her room. When she got inside, she immediately sat at the table and laid the envelope in front of her. But as she looked at it, the thought occurred to her that someone had to have known she'd gotten cider or they wouldn't have delivered the next envelope. Had someone been watching her and Nick? A shiver ran down her spine. Or had they just guessed that she'd get some today? Perhaps that was it, she reasoned.

She ran her fingertips over the wax seal. Who was it? And why was this happening to her? Whatever the reason, the trip had brought her to Nick. And now, she wasn't sure which she was more excited about—sharing a car with him to the airport or getting this letter.

With a deep breath, she picked off the seal, opened the envelope, then pulled out the note and read it.

I'll bet you can't remember where we got the cider? (I knew you'd be asking yourself that.) It's because you'd stopped into a shop to look at candles, and I popped out to get us each a cup. I never understood your fascination with balls of wax that you light on fire, but I loved the way your face lit up when you got that new one that day. I didn't send you to the orchard for the cider. I sent you to get you doing things new to you. The orchard is your new place, somewhere I've never been. I hope you find more spots just for you. I also hope you had a great trip and made some memories that you can take home with you. When you get home, something will be waiting for you.

Tears brimmed in her eyes and goose bumps rose on her skin. She'd had almost that same thought about making new memories when she was enjoying her pie. How could Toby know that?

While she hadn't recalled the cider that day, she did remember the candle.

❄

"Smell it!" She'd chased him down the sidewalk with the open jar in one hand and her cider in the other as he pretended to be repulsed.

"It'll make me sneeze." He put his hand over his mouth and nose.

"This one won't. The scent is subtle." She fumbled the jar shut, dropped it into the bag, and attempted to pry his fingers off his face, but he was too strong for her.

"There's only one way you'll get my hand off my nose," he said.

"And what is that?"

They stood in the middle of the sidewalk while people maneuvered around them.

"Kiss me."

She playfully rolled her eyes and then she pushed herself up onto her toes. Gently, he put his hand on her face and drew her in. His lips met hers delicately.

"This scent is way better than that ol' candle."

❄

She blinked the tears away, the memory having dropped into her mind like a heavy weight. These notes were definitely from Toby—there was no question at this point. How was he doing this? Someone had to be delivering them, right? As much as Toby worried about privacy, wouldn't he also know she'd be a nervous wreck at the thought of someone waiting around in the shadows, giving her the notes? There was no other way to make it happen, right? He could've organized these last few with the hotel, but had he also prearranged all the others to be at the locations where she'd received them? And had he guessed the exact times and dates she'd arrive at each spot, all while unable to leave his bed? And then there was the situation with the white SUV... It wasn't as if Toby himself were able to come back to life and drive away at top speed. She got up and looked through the peephole, checking to see if anyone was lurking. The coast was clear.

Her mind reeling, she called Marion.

"How was the work party?" Heather asked.

"Decent. Good cocktails, boring company—apart from Anthony. He and I actually enjoyed ourselves."

"That's good."

"It's easy to do when we don't mention the elephant in the room. I adore him, but our opposing views on that specific subject are too large to overcome long term, and I still don't know what to do. I have to choose my love for him or a future family. That's an impossible choice. And I'm angry that he didn't let me know this so we could figure it out *before* we got married." She let out a sigh. "But we have a therapy session scheduled after the holiday, so there's that."

"I really hope you two can find common ground."

"Yeah... But enough about my drama, what's up with you?"

Heather told her all about her day.

"Someone delivered the note while Nick and I were at the orchard," she explained to her friend. "To get it up here, and know what room number to leave it at, I think it would have to be planned through the hotel staff."

"Have you asked them if they could tell you who was delivering the notes?"

"They didn't know who it was. They said it could have been a courier."

"Mm." Her disappointment came down the line. "I wonder if you'll ever know."

"I have no idea, but it's killing me. I don't understand how Toby could've done all this and been so precise while he was sick. It's so unbelievable that I find myself believing in miracles."

"That's not a bad thing. So how was your day with Nick?"

"It was really great. Like, unusually great. I like him."

A high-pitched squeal came from the other end of the line. "That's fabulous. I've been waiting for you to find someone wonderful. You deserve happiness. And right at Christmastime too. As if he was handed to you with a big bow on his head—maybe miracles do exist. When can I meet him?"

"I only just met him," she said with a laugh. "Maybe give me a couple more days."

"I can whip up a double date in minutes. Believe me, Anthony and I would love the diversion."

"I'll let you know."

The idea of going public with any kind of relationship was daunting. She'd have to eventually tell Nick about who she was. She wasn't the famous one, and her life went on pretty uneventfully, so hopefully he'd be okay with it and take a few media mentions in stride. Once they'd landed, she'd give him her number and see how things progressed. Then if they got serious, she'd tell him everything.

She told Marion she'd check in again later and opened her journal.

What have you cooked up, Toby? How are you doing this? While I love the gesture, I'm also struggling with it. I wouldn't be out doing all these new things without you, but just when I'm starting to move forward, your next note pulls me back to my old life, and I miss you all over again. My heart can hardly handle the push and pull. While I love the idea of moving forward, and I'm open to loving again, I can't quite get myself to commit, and your letters make that struggle a bit harder. I miss you so much.

She closed the journal, got ready for bed early, and called in room service for dinner. Then she crawled into bed.

Would she have to wait until she saw Toby again at the end of her life to find out how he'd done all this? There was a time when she'd hoped that day would come sooner rather than later, but now, she wasn't so sure. Nick had a hand in changing her mind. And, while she was still getting used to the idea of moving on, she couldn't wait to see where things went next with him.

She'd told him she'd meet him in the lobby tomorrow at nine, to head to the airport. He'd said he'd have a car waiting for them. Then they'd be off, "back to reality," as he said. But what would that reality look like when she got back and woke up every morning in the apartment she'd shared with Toby? What would the New Year bring? Despite her trepidation, an unusual sort of hope had taken hold, and she was actually excited to find out. Sure, there was a part of her that worried about how she might handle another relationship, about whether she'd be ready if things moved along. But she'd never know until she took the plunge. And while she didn't have it all planned out, very carefully, she was going to take the next step.

Chapter Fourteen

After checking out of her room, Heather met Nick in the lobby. He was holding two paper coffee cups, his coat draped over his arm. He handed her one, and as he got close, she noticed how his oatmeal-colored sweater brought out the green in his eyes.

"I ran to the shop down the road and got you a honey latte. I remembered you ordered one at the restaurant."

"Thank you." She couldn't deny the fizzle of happiness that he'd remembered such a small detail about her. "How thoughtful."

He grinned at her. "It's cold out there. You'll need it." He rolled his bag over from beside the front desk first and then took her large suitcase for her. He opened the door, ushering her into the icy air before rolling her bag outside.

As promised, he had a car waiting. The driver hoisted their bags into the trunk, and she climbed in. Then they were off.

"Sleep okay?" Nick asked as the car inched its way into traffic.

"Surprisingly well, thanks to you."

"To me?" He tapped his chest.

"I don't think this trip would've been the same without you. I had a lot of fun, for the first time in a long time."

"I'm glad to hear that." The fondness he exuded toward her took her breath away.

They settled into a comfortable quiet, and the driver filled the silence with small talk, but her mind was busy. How unexpected that she was in her lowest state during the holiday, and Nick had dropped in like some sort of Christmas gift. If someone had asked her only a few days ago if she was ready for even one date, she'd have run in the other direction. But now, she was thinking of all the things she and Nick could do together after they returned home. She liked the slow way he'd made friends with her and then the gentle build of affection. It was natural and undeniable.

Was this the beginning of something incredible? With the dawn of a new day and a fresh perspective, she wondered if Toby could be working on her life from up above. Was that possible? He'd certainly want her to be happy, and it would be just like him to create something magical for her. Did he have the Big Man's ear upstairs after all?

When they pulled up outside the airport, Nick helped her check in her bags and they walked together to their gate. A few minutes later, they were boarding the same flight, and just as before, he sat beside her.

As she took her window seat, she couldn't stop thinking about how much had changed. Instead of both of them avoiding the shared armrest, he'd let her have it, and the tips of her fingers brushed his arm again, but neither of them pulled away. And to give room to the elderly woman who'd taken the aisle seat on the other side of him, Nick leaned slightly in Heather's direction, which she didn't mind at all.

A pang of sadness shot through her that this was their final hour together and then the world would filter back in. While they'd see each other after, their regular lives would compete for their time. She'd have to fight the urge to spend every minute with him, avoid the fact that he was her lifeline to a better future, so she could do the mundane things like get to work on time. Maybe it was for the best. She did need to be able to depend on herself for contentment before she fell for anyone.

Slow and steady. Maybe they could see each other once every couple of weeks at first and then progress to every week, and if they hit it off, she'd let him come over during the week and he could introduce her to Ophelia.

They turned their devices onto airplane mode and tucked them into their bags. She wouldn't need a phone or her book for this flight. She wanted to give Nick her undivided attention. The flight attendants performed their safety demonstrations, and the plane maneuvered to the runway. Before long, they were in the air.

"What's the first thing you'll do when you get home?" she asked him.

"Pick up Ophelia from the neighbor's and take her for a walk and a Tail Wagger."

"A Tail Wagger?" She giggled.

"Basically, an overpriced paper cup of whipped cream sprinkled with ground dog treats from the local coffee shop. But it's her favorite thing to do and the only way she'll get over me leaving her for two days. She's such a diva."

Heather laughed.

"What about you?" he asked.

"I'll probably call my best friend, Marion. I've been giving her a play-by-play of the trip, and I'll want to fill her in on the plane ride home."

That interest flickered. "What will you tell her?"

"Maybe something about the really awesome guy who sat next to me."

The corners of his mouth twitched upward. "Awesome?"

"Hopefully. I'm setting the stage for you to entertain me for the next hour and fifteen minutes."

He chuckled. "No pressure."

Their banter made her want to know more about him. "So you went to Belmont and then got a job as a researcher?" she asked.

"Pretty much." He shifted slightly toward her, making eye contact. "I graduated with an MFA in creative writing and a minor in sociology, which without an added degree or concentration, greatly narrowed my corporate choices."

She nodded. Having spent time in the creative world with Toby, she could understand the struggle. Most of the songwriters in their circles had made ends meet with other jobs before they'd hit it big with their writing.

"I worked for a while as a copywriter, and I wrote a few grants for another company—freelance, but I struggled to get my foot in the door anywhere. After quite the struggle to find where I fit in the industry, I finally found my current job as a research writer."

That glimmer surfaced, making her stomach flip.

"Sometimes, I get to create presentations and marketing copy, which can be entertaining. It definitely isn't the wide-open, inspired endeavor I was hoping for when I'd gotten a creative writing degree, but when I'm between projects, it allows me the evening hours to do what I really love, which is write creatively."

She swallowed her surprise. Under all that research, he was a creative. Toby's writing came to mind. He loved nothing more than to sit in their bay window with his guitar, scratching away on his notepad.

"What do you write in your off time?" She was almost afraid to ask for fear that he'd say songwriting. A part of her liked the fact that Nick was so different from Toby—more talkative, animated, ready to share so much of himself.

"I've dabbled in fiction and a few nonfiction projects, but I haven't published anything."

Her shoulders relaxed. "So books?"

"Yeah. But lately, I haven't been able to do as much writing as I want to. Maybe I will when I get home." He smiled at her.

Had she inspired him in the same way he'd impacted her?

The flight attendants announced the beverage and snack service, and he put his tray down.

"How about you?" he asked. "Is being a librarian what you've always wanted to do?"

An answer bubbled up, marking this moment as the time when she could tell him about Toby. It was the perfect segue. Should she? After so many years being closed up, she struggled to know the answer. Eventually, she'd have to if they went any further, so it might make sense to do it now, rip off the Band-Aid.

Summoning all her courage, she cleared her throat. "Actually, no. I was married and didn't work before."

He blinked.

Keep going. Tell him.

"My husband was a songwriter," she said quietly, her words only loud enough to fill the small space between them. "He died of cancer, and I had to go back to work. Maybe you know him? Toby Hart."

He blinked again. His breathing seemed shallow.

She'd clearly made him nervous. Had her connection to Toby been too much of a surprise? She'd effectively just yanked them both into reality. If he did know who Toby was, he'd probably heard about his death, which would bring up a whole lot of questions about her. It had only been a year. He might be wondering if he'd have to deal with navigating her grief. He could even be thinking about the press's reaction to anything that might come of this. Tears wanted to well up for the broken woman she'd been before this trip and the tiny wisp of a new woman who'd begun to emerge. While she didn't want to ruin what she and Nick had started, she had to tell him eventually.

"Have you heard of him?" she asked, hoping her question would prompt some explanation as to what he was feeling.

"Yes." The empathetic drop in his features revealed that her emotions had surfaced despite her attempt to keep them at bay. "I'm so sorry."

That was the most common response she'd gotten over the last year, whenever anyone found out about Toby's death. It was a nice, even reply when they didn't know what else to say.

"You're incredibly strong," he said suddenly.

Strong wasn't even close to the descriptors she'd given herself in the last year. "I look strong to you?"

He nodded. "Losing a loved one is an immense weight to carry, and you do it effortlessly. This is the first time all weekend I've seen an inkling of that weight in your eyes."

"Maybe I'm getting practiced at carrying it." *Or maybe you lift it off me*, she wanted to say.

The flight attendant took their drink orders, but Nick's attention was right back on Heather the minute the attendant had moved on.

"I feel stronger after having met you," she said, trying to find the best way to say it. "You've made a huge impact in helping me to carry it." Her absolute vulnerability scared her. She hadn't talked about her personal life with anyone but Marion, and revealing her bruised and battered underbelly wasn't entirely comfortable. More so because she worried about Nick's thoughts in all this. He'd met her on a quick weekend trip, he hadn't signed up for her baggage.

"I know that's probably weird to say after only two days," she added, trying to sound less crazy. What was she doing unloading all this on him?

But he offered a gentle smile. "*I've* helped you?"

"Well, I actually came on this trip to feel closer to Toby." She quietly recounted to him all the notes and what had happened.

He listened, his face void of judgment.

"I know getting notes after someone's passed on sounds insane. I hear myself. And I have no answer for it all."

"You have no idea who might be doing all this?" he asked.

She shook her head. "Maybe you could help me try to figure it out, given your research skills."

He laughed. "I didn't say I was an investigative researcher. I mostly look at marketing trends."

True to the nature she'd witnessed all weekend, he took all her drama in stride, seemingly unruffled and relaxed. She craved the way he balanced her slight edge. And she couldn't deny how great he was for her.

Chapter Fifteen

The plane landed, but this time, Heather and Nick walked together to the baggage claim to retrieve their bags.

"Do you have a ride home?" he asked.

"My car's in the lot," she replied, hoping he needed a ride himself. "How about you?"

"A friend's picking me up."

This was it. Back to reality indeed. She pulled out her phone. "Give me your number."

He told her the number, and she created a contact.

His phone pinged. "My ride's outside already, so I have to go." He shifted his bag on his shoulder and tipped his suitcase onto the rolling wheels.

"Okay." Feeling rushed all of a sudden, she said, "I'll text you when I get to my car so you can have mine."

They lingered briefly, unsure of how to leave one another. Should she give him a hug? Just say goodbye? Nothing quite fit.

She waved her phone in the air. "I'll text you."

"Sounds good." He took a step into her personal space. "Thank you," he said. "It was fun."

"Yes, it was." She smiled up at him.

"I'll see you soon, yes?"

Her heart pattered. "Definitely."

He flashed that million-dollar smile and then turned around and headed for the exit.

And with that, her whirlwind weekend was over. With a sigh, she took her bags and made her way to the shuttle that would take her to her car. As soon as she got her bags into the trunk and started her engine, she sent a text to Nick, telling him it was her and that she hoped he got home okay. She told him to text her whenever he wanted to meet up. Then she bit her lip and hit send, already missing him.

A relatively uneventful drive later, she stopped to unlock her mailbox on her way upstairs. Another red-and-white envelope was nestled among her mail. Toby's last message floated into her mind: *Something will be waiting for you...*

When she got upstairs, she set the mail on the counter and purposely waited to open the envelope until she got settled. Using the residual calm she'd built up that weekend, she took her time unpacking, making a laundry pile next to the washer and dryer, and stowing her bags in the closet. She showered and slipped on the comfy tracksuit and fuzzy socks she liked to wear around the house. Then she clicked on the lights of her Christmas tree and gazed at it, finally taking it in. Until now, she hadn't paid a lot of attention to it. But after this weekend, she began to see that, broken or not, this was her life, and she needed to make it into something. She ran a finger over the little guitar ornament—one of Toby's choices.

Her phone rang. Marion.

"How was the flight?"

"Amazing."

"Spill! Anthony's working on his legal presentation for tomorrow, and I'm dying to hear all about your trip."

"Have you had dinner?" Heather asked. "I'm starving."

"I have lasagna leftovers. Want me to bring some over?" Marion asked.

"That actually sounds amazing. I have nothing in my fridge."

"I'm already on my way."

She was falling back into real life easily. But now, a tiny seed of hope had begun to sprout. "Too late to ask you to bring wine?"

"It's already in the bag."

She grinned. "See you in a few."

She got off the phone and lit a candle on the coffee table. When she did, the last note from Toby, mentioning candles, came to mind. She went to the counter, fished the envelope out of the pile, and opened it. Inside was a note and a bookmark with the logo of an old secondhand bookshop called Between the Stacks that she and Toby had visited.

> I hope you had an enjoyable weekend. The fun isn't over. I've got something waiting for you at the bookshop.

They'd been to Between the Stacks more times than she could recount. There wasn't one particular event from the bookshop that stood out, but she had fond memories of all the times they'd visited together. What was most noticeable about this location was the absolute happiness she had felt doing the mundane with Toby. Nothing spectacular had occurred in the shop, but the way he'd put his hand on her back when they were looking through the books, or the quiet whispers in her ear while she was reading, was enough to sustain her for a lifetime. And she longed to have a real exchange of affection like that again.

She set the note on the counter and placed the bookmark on top. "Toby, can you hear me at all?"

As always, silence followed her question.

Not too long after, the door buzzed, and she let Marion in.

"It's only been a weekend, but it feels like ages since we had our snowy girls' night." Marion gave her a hug and then put the leftovers in the kitchen. "I can't wait to hear all about your trip."

Heather preheated the oven. "The weekend was so surprising." As she emptied the carrier bag of lasagna and French bread, she handed Marion a corkscrew for the wine and filled her in on everything she hadn't been able to tell her on the phone.

Marion opened the bottle. "You positively glow when you talk about him."

Heather bit back a grin and set two wine glasses on the counter. "It's crazy, right? Last time you and I were together, I was wallowing in grief, watching my wedding video and wondering how my life would ever progress beyond that. Nick moved the needle in a matter of days. How did he do it?"

Marion filled their glasses. "Because you two were meant to be, obviously. You have an absolutely dreamy look on your face."

"I'm still pretty delicate. I do worry that I might not recover if he broke my heart. I've already thought about it."

Marion handed her a glass. "Take things slowly. Has he texted you back yet?"

"Not yet, but he had to get home and pick up his dog. He walks her to the coffee shop and gets her a whipped-cream treat. It's so cute."

"And he might not want to look too eager. You two are

still in early days; you're both playing the dating game of being head over heels while trying not to be clingy."

Heather took a slow sip of chardonnay and swallowed. "I don't want to play games. I just want to enjoy each other."

"Give it a little time. You'll get there." Marion held up her glass. "To Christmas miracles."

"Miracles indeed," Heather said with a laugh.

"Speaking of miracles, have you gotten any new letters from Toby?"

"I did." She grabbed the note and the bookmark and handed them to Marion. "He wants me to go this bookshop."

Marion looked down at the letter. "Intriguing." She handed them back.

"Here's the thing: There's no way Toby could actually be doing this. And Nick is more real life than these notes from the past." Heather waved the letter between them. "While I adore reliving the little memories of my time with Toby, it's strangely keeping me closer to a time in my life that I can't return to. I'm not sure what to do about it."

"You don't have to go to the bookstore."

Heather placed the letter back on the counter and they went into the living room and settled on the sofa. "The thing is, I owe it to Toby's memory to follow through with the notes until I can figure out who's writing them and why."

"I'm always here for you if you need me. I don't mind taking road trips to follow the letters," Marion said. "The excitement is a nice diversion from my own issues."

"Thanks."

"And if you want me to come, we can never go wrong with book shopping," Marion said with a wiggle and then sipped her wine. "But I think the car chase might have been my favorite. I felt like James Bond."

"I wonder if we'll ever catch the driver," Heather said with a laugh.

Marion's eyebrows bounced with enthusiasm.

That hope took hold once more. "Christmas is only three days away. We should do some Christmas activities and share in the spirit of the season. I'd like to do something to make a difference for people, in Toby's memory. We should bake cookies and go downtown and give them to the homeless or something."

Marion brightened. "Oh, I'd *love* to do that. What made you think of it?"

"With Toby's notes, I've been feeling caught between reality and heaven. Toby gave so much to people through his charity work. It got me thinking about that verse my mom used to read me in Hebrews that said not to forget to show hospitality to strangers, for by doing so, some people have entertained angels without knowing it. Toby loved that verse too. Maybe somehow, he'll be watching."

Marion put her hand to her chest. "Oh, I love that so much. Just tell me when."

The oven timer went off. Heather set her wine on the coffee table, and Marion trailed her into the kitchen.

"We could deliver cookies tomorrow and then go to the bookshop." Heather retrieved her oven mitts from the drawer and took out the steaming lasagna. The savory scent of garlic and onions filled the tiny kitchen. "What if we made them 'Hope Bags'? I just came up with that."

"Oh, I like the sound of it. Tell me more." Marion put her glass on the island.

"We could put some basic necessities in a bag, maybe add an inspirational verse and cookies." Heather sank a serving spoon into the bubbling, cheesy lasagna.

Marion bit her lip excitedly. "Anthony's got that presentation tomorrow, so we could bake and fill bags at my house if you want to."

Heather took off her mitts and clapped her hands. “Say no more. What time?”

“Want to get an early start? I could probably meet at nine.”

“I’ll pick up some supplies and come to you.” Heather took two plates over and set the table. With the smell of dinner and the candle burning in the living room, the whole place had a cozy, nostalgic feel.

Marion shook her head. “Who are you after this weekend? While I’ve always adored you, you’ve got this bright light inside you that wasn’t there before.”

“I can’t help but feel like I’m turning a corner.”

“Turn, girl!” Marion took her hand and gave her a spin, the two of them giggling next to the glimmer of Christmas lights.

Chapter Sixteen

Marion lived in a rancher, tucked away on a side street in the city, far enough from the hustle and bustle to feel as though they were in the suburbs, but close enough to be downtown in a matter of minutes. Heather pulled up at 9 a.m. sharp. She carried a bag of baking ingredients and Hope Bag supplies to the front door and rang the bell. Scarlett casually peered out at her from a nearby windowsill.

Marion opened the door and the cat vanished from view, reappearing at Heather's leg with a purr. Marion took the bags from Heather, who bent down and stroked the kitten's little head.

"I've been thinking about this project all morning," Marion said, ushering her inside past the entryway table full of Christmas cards from loved ones. "I have a pile of combs, tissues, and lip balm for each bag."

"Those are perfect. I got toothbrushes, travel toothpaste, and soap."

Heather followed her past a stout Christmas tree adorned

with hand-tied red ribbons and various ornaments that she recognized were given to Marion by students in their library classes over the years. The corner next to the kitchen held a cozy reading chair, the walls behind it lined with books.

While Marion was the least organized of the two of them, she won the award for the coziest home. Everything in it meant something. Heather only wished she could have that one day. After losing Toby, she hadn't taken care of filling her home with thoughtful items. Even the tree had been out of obligation, to keep her in the present.

She stripped off her coat and hung it on a kitchen chair. Marion put her bag on the counter and began unpacking it, adding the items to the ingredients already out and the list of what they'd need. They'd decided on chocolate chip cookies and sugar cookies, with a few macaroons thrown in.

Baking had been Toby's domain. Heather stepped into the task with resolution, another new undertaking to add to her changing perspective, thanks to her weekend with Nick.

"We've got all-purpose flour, granulated sugar," Marion said, ticking off her list, "brown sugar, unsalted butter, eggs, vanilla extract, baking powder, baking soda, salt, chocolate chips, oil, and sweetened shredded coconut..."

"I wonder when would be a good time to call Nick," Heather said, her thoughts spilling out into the open. "How long should I wait?"

Marion put down the pad of paper. "He hasn't called yet?"

"No, but it's only morning, and we got in yesterday afternoon—he does have a life, even if I don't."

"I resent that," Marion said with a smirk, before bending down and retrieving a mixing bowl from a lower cabinet.

"You know what I mean." She paused. "So when *should* I call him?"

Marion set two batter stirrers on the counter. "Wait for him to call you."

"Really? Why?"

"Because—and I say this with love—I already see how much you're depending on this. You're literally hanging on every move he makes. You *can* be happy without him. Push yourself."

Heather blew air through her lips. "Gosh, you're right. I only just met him, and I already feel like he's some sort of link to a new life. Ugh. He doesn't need that kind of pressure, and I have to learn to stand on my own two feet." She leaned on the counter. "The problem is that I had such a great time with him. I didn't think I was capable of enjoying myself like that anymore. And after the year I've had, I crave that feeling again."

"I hear you. But you don't want to rush headfirst into a relationship. If things don't work out, it could crush you. Maybe let the sensation of happiness linger for a while. Then, when he calls, you'll be ready to take things slowly."

"You're such a wonderful voice of reason."

"I'm going to hold you to that statement the next time we have a faculty dress-up day and I offer my suggestions."

"No." She pointed at Marion. "We're not doing Book Character Sound-Effect Day. Can you imagine how loud a school full of kids making all that noise would be? Nightmare."

"It would be fuuuuun. And the kids would remember it forever."

"But we'd all lose our hearing, and we kind of need that."

"It's so much more original than dress-up day." She offered a long, slow blink to emphasize her point.

"Dress-up day works. The kids learn the characters, read the books, and they get to wear something memorable."

Marion rolled her eyes playfully and handed Heather a measuring spoon.

❄

By late afternoon, they were walking down Broadway, handing out cellophane bags of cookies and hygiene items tied with red bows to those in need. Heather was filled with a quiet sense of purpose as the weight of each small exchange settled gently in her chest. Weary smiles and brief thank-yous made the cold air feel warmer, and even the silences carried a sense of shared humanity. She was able to handle another task that used to be led by Toby: giving to the less fortunate at Christmastime. Each interaction conveyed an unexpected gravity, as if the moment mattered more than the object itself—to both of them.

By the end, their hands were empty and their noses cold, but their hearts were full. In a way, she felt as if she were standing next to Toby—heaven and earth side by side.

Marion put her arm around her. "Ready to hit the bookstore?"

"Yeah," she said, feeling joyful.

Heather drove to the secondhand bookshop across town. Between the Stacks occupied a narrow brick storefront shaded by an old maple, its windows crowded with handwritten signs and sun-faded paperbacks piled like leaning towers.

Heather opened the door for Marion, and they went inside. A bell above the door chimed gently. The air smelled of dust, black coffee, and thyme. The wooden floors creaked softly beneath their feet as they walked.

Shelves leaned, overfilled with dog-eared novels, forgotten biographies, and music histories that felt right at home in the city—Toby's favorite genre to browse. He'd been the one to find this place, and whenever they went they spent hours sifting through all the books, often leaving with armfuls of obscure titles that they'd spend the next month devouring quietly next to one another. She loved those shared moments of being lost in a story, only to surface at the sensation of Toby's touch as he trailed a finger along her hand mindlessly, his nose in his book.

Light filtered through the front windows, warming a pair of mismatched armchairs where readers lingered, as if the outside world had agreed to wait. Perhaps that was why Toby had brought her here—to slow down, take her time, and get lost for a while.

"Are we looking for a specific shelf or what?" Marion asked.

"The note didn't say. I guess I'll go up and ask the sales clerk." Then, she put a hand on Marion's arm. "But let's take our time. Want to look around?"

"Um... We're in a *book*store. Yes. I'm more than happy to dawdle."

They wandered slowly through the shop. It was like being pulled back in time. Heather trailed her fingers along the spines as if reading by touch alone. The tactile act of browsing was one of the things that had drawn her to reading as a child. All her life, she'd loved nothing more than to slide books in and out of their places, the back cover blurb a hidden treasure offering just enough to make her wonder. Given his talent for songwriting, Toby had shared the same interest in books, focusing on contemporary poetry or memoirs. The two of them would spend much of their day in silence, yet they were so connected by their mutual respect for reading that they felt as close as if they'd been chatting all day.

Creased paperbacks, clothbound hardcovers, and titles that had landed there by chance rather than design—every trip to this shop offered a new surprise. Time loosened its grip even further as she paused to skim a paragraph here, a dedication there. When she'd visited with Toby, and he'd been an aisle over, the soft sound of his pages flipping through the stacks had given her a sense of calm unlike anything else.

"Looking through all these feels less like shopping and more like listening," Heather said, lost in the task of finding her unique prize. "It's as if they all have something to say."

"Yeah," Marion said, grabbing a third book to pile into her arms. "In my case, they're all shouting at me like an oversized litter of puppies. I need to take them aaaall home."

When they'd whittled down their choices to a few solid reads, they took their selections up to the counter to check out. A man with a cable-knit sweater and gray hair at his temples greeted them at the register. He rang up Marion and then Heather and put the books into their respective bags.

When he handed Heather hers, she leaned in. "This might sound crazy, but do you happen to have a red-and-white envelope waiting for someone named Heather Hart?"

His bushy eyebrows raised. "I do. A man dropped it by yesterday." He offered a mischievous smile. "Is this some sort of holiday scavenger hunt?"

"Sort of. He didn't tell you anything about who he is, did he?"

The man frowned and shook his head. "Sorry, he didn't. He just walked in and said he was doing something special for someone for Christmas and a woman named Heather might come by asking for it. Then he handed me the envelope and asked if I'd keep it until you arrived. He bought a book and left." The man reached under the counter to retrieve the note for her.

"Okay, thanks." She took the envelope. "What book did he buy?"

The man frowned. "I can't remember. Maybe nonfiction?"

Heather nodded, trying to avoid the feeling that she might never get to the end of all this. “It wasn’t a memoir, was it?”

“I’m not sure.” He smiled at her. “Merry Christmas,” he said.

“Merry Christmas.”

With her books in hand, Heather walked out to her car with no more answers than she’d had before.

Chapter Seventeen

As she was opening her car door, Heather's phone rang in her handbag, sending her heart a patter. "That could be Nick." She jumped into the car, tossed her bag of books into the backseat, and dug around for her phone.

Sure it had to be on its final ring, she answered it quickly without looking at the screen. "Hello?" she said, breathless.

"Hi, this is Alex Branson from *People's Entertainment*. I tried to call you a while ago, but we were somehow disconnected."

Yeah. She'd hung up. She was about to again, but Nick's easygoing nature came to mind. Until now, she'd bristled at the mention of a reporter. She didn't need to anymore. She just had to tell them what she wanted and didn't want. After seeing how Nick was with people, conversation with others felt easier.

Marion mouthed, "Is it him?"

Heather frowned and shook her head, then returned to the call. "Sorry we got disconnected. But now's not really a good time."

"When should I call you back?" he asked.

"You'd be wasting your time trying to talk to me. Toby and I made the decision to keep his life out of the spotlight and his death entirely private. I have no comment on the success of the album, if that's what you're after."

"Maybe we could grab a coffee or something—off the record—at a better time."

That was weird. Why would he want to do that? "I'll think about it," she said, although she already knew the answer. There was no way she'd meet a random journalist for coffee when she'd already told him she wasn't talking. Maybe later, when she had more time, she could find out for curiosity's sake. "Can you check back in a few days?"

"Of course. Have a nice evening."

"Thank you. You too." She hung up the phone and turned to an ogling Marion.

"Are you really going to talk to a reporter?"

"Definitely not. But I wanted to get him off the call so I could open the note." She tossed her phone into her handbag and picked the envelope up off her lap, waving it in the air.

Marion clapped her hands in tiny taps. "This is all so exciting."

With a giggle, Heather slipped her finger under the wax seal and pulled out a single sheet of paper. She read:

Roses are red, violets are blue, the florist who made your wedding bouquet has something for you. Hey, even I slip into a cliché now and then. I do my best. Anyway, ask for Rachel.

"If you want to go right now, I'm happy to ride along.

What's the name of the florist?" Marion was already pulling up her navigation app.

"It's called Stemhouse." The mental image of her bouquet of pink roses lying in the sand in her wedding video floated into her mind. That memory and the note made her feel as if Toby were in the car with them.

Marion tapped her screen at lightning speed. "Seventeen minutes away. What do you think?"

"Let's do it."

Marion pumped her fist in the air.

"Why are you so fired up?" Heather asked, amused.

"Because I might get another car chase out of this."

Heather threw back her head and laughed. "Not with me driving. I drive like an old lady."

Marion's shoulders dropped. "True."

They made the quiet drive to Stemhouse. Marion flicked through the radio stations while Heather slipped into thoughts about Nick. What was he doing right now? Probably walking Ophelia or having a late lunch at one of the little cafés, tapping away on his laptop while the dog slept at his feet. Could he be checking his phone to see if she'd called, deliberating on when was too early to call her? Given how quickly they'd hit it off, it felt as though he should have at least wanted to text her back to say he got her number. Perhaps he'd try to call tonight.

His warm smile and playful green eyes filled her mind. She'd never met anyone like him. He was so comfortable in his own skin, it was intoxicating. She only wished she could be that relaxed. But he had rubbed off on her. She'd handled the reporter from *People's Entertainment* with ease when those calls used to rattle her.

She came to a stop outside Stemhouse. The elegant floral boutique stood on the outskirts of Nashville like a well-kept secret, its unimposing facade softened by climbing greenery.

They got out of the car and went inside, the little bells on the door jingling to announce their entrance.

A woman came from the back and greeted them. "Let me know if you're looking for anything special."

"Thank you," Heather returned. She didn't want to rush up to the counter just yet. Instead, she took her time, drinking in the Christmas cheer of the place.

Evergreen garlands draped the shelves, their scent of fresh pine, citrus, and clove filling the air. Hand-tied wreaths and seasonal centerpieces had been crafted with thoughtful detail, balancing tradition with a modern, understated charm. She ran her hand along the clay vases that lined the shelves and admired the blooms in Christmas colors. Light filtered through the tall windows, catching on eucalyptus stems and garden roses, while the air carried a subtle scent of earth and perfume. It was as though they had stepped out of the city's rhythm and into a slower, more thoughtful world, where every flower arrangement seemed to speak tiny truths from her past.

One memory of her and Toby came flooding back.

❄

"I'm thinking we should do roses," she said, browsing the shelves of wildflowers. "What do you think?"

He wrapped his arms around her from behind, moved her hair off her shoulder, and kissed her neck, despite the prying eyes of the woman at the counter.

"Seriously, are you okay with roses?"

He chuckled. "I couldn't care less what you hold for that hour as long as I get to take you home." He scooped her up, making her squeal.

The woman behind the counter sighed happily.

❄

"You should get a bouquet to take home," Marion said, fiddling with a little bunch of red roses. "They're all so beautiful."

"Maybe I will."

Heather went over to the other wall and perused arrangements that featured velvety amaryllis, hellebore, and winter berries gathered in muted, elegant palettes. Each one paired miniature evergreens with soft winter blooms, berries, and subtle accents of dried elements. No two bouquets were exactly alike, yet together they formed a cohesive display that felt warm and personal. They seemed perfect for her coffee table back home. She settled on a three-rose bundle with fir sprigs and berries.

"That's gorgeous," Marion said. "Makes me want to get one."

"Maybe you should."

"I'll just admire yours. Scarlett would have it all over the floor in less than an hour."

With a laugh, Heather went up to the counter and paid for the bouquet. "I was told to ask for Rachel."

"That's my name," the woman said.

"Oh, hi." Heather smiled. "Do you have an envelope for me? My name's Heather Hart."

"Yes, I sure do." With a sparkle in her eye, the woman retrieved the familiar envelope from the back.

They thanked her and left the store.

"Two letters in one day—that's exciting," Marion said as Heather used the seat belt in the backseat to keep her bouquet safe on the ride home.

"It's incredible." She got into the driver's seat and fastened her seat belt. "I just don't understand how Toby's doing it."

"It's a pretty amazing Christmas gift," Marion said, blowing into her hands.

Heather tried to smile, but her thoughts must have shown on the outside.

"You don't think so?" Marion asked.

Heather started the car to get some heat going and then twisted toward Marion. "There's a part of me that wants to hang out in my memories of Toby all day, but there's another part that's ready to move on. I don't want to leave Toby but, rather, carry his memory with me so I can get on with my life." She shook her head, looking down at the envelope in her lap. "I don't want to seem ungrateful, because he was the most thoughtful person on the planet, but when I get another letter that pulls me back into my old life, I'm pulled somewhere I can't return to."

Marion's face creased with contemplation. "I wish I'd known the Toby that swept you off your feet. But from what you've told me over the last year, Toby was a lot of things, but random was not a characteristic you ever mentioned. He loved you, and he's building that message in an elaborate way—the true mark of a great songwriter." She smiled.

"You're right." Heather waved the envelope in the air. "Maybe he'll fill me in on how he managed this right here."

"Maybe!"

Heather ripped open the envelope and pulled out the next note. When she did, a key fell from the folded paper, and she scrambled to keep it from going down between the seats. When she inspected it, she knew what it was immediately, and she smiled. *So Toby had it?*

Are you tired of running around yet? I knew you'd be holed up in that apartment this Christmas, probably wallowing, so I wanted to get you out into the world. But now, you get to kick back. I've got one more place to send you. Tomorrow, I want you to pack your things and drive to the family cabin. I always wanted to take you there one last time so we could enjoy all the renovations, and I never got the chance.

"Tell me what it says. I'm dying over here," Marion said.

"It's the key to the family cabin," she replied, more to her own introspection than to Marion's question. "It's in Wears Valley—over three hours' drive away."

Marion looked at her in confusion. "You have a cabin?"

She ran her finger over the address printed at the bottom of the note. "It's Toby's. He inherited it from his grandparents. It sits on a mountaintop overlooking the valley. We renovated it with some of the money he got from his first big royalty payout, but we never had time to visit. As it was, we didn't go enough, even before the renovations. We thought we were so busy... If only we'd slowed down."

"Wears Valley—that sounds wonderful."

"I wish you could go with me, but I know tomorrow's Christmas Eve."

"Yeah, I'd have a hard time convincing Anthony to let me have a girls' trip on the biggest holiday of the year. Probably wouldn't look too good, given our attempt to work through our issues." She twisted toward her. "Think you'll be okay out there by yourself?"

"He wouldn't send me if it wasn't safe, right?"

Marion sucked in a breath. "Wait a minute. Remember, we're *assuming* Toby set all this up. But what if he didn't—can I remind you of that possibility? I'm not crazy about the idea of you being all alone in some remote cabin in the woods.

Especially on Christmas when everything's closed and people are all with their families. The town will be empty. It sounds like an abduction plot if you ask me."

"Thank you for that. I feel much better about going now," she said, the sarcasm heavy.

"The whole thing doesn't sit well with me."

"If someone wanted to abduct me, they could've done it in South Carolina—or anywhere along the way—but they didn't. And when we tried to chase their car, they fled. I think I'll be fine."

"It weirds me out that the white-SUV guy probably knows you'll be there." Marion made a face. "But it's your call."

❄

After dropping Marion at home, and picking up a sandwich for dinner, Heather returned to her apartment. She set the flower arrangement on the coffee table in the living room then stood there for a long time without really seeing the bouquet, her mind swirling.

If it was Toby sending the notes, which she was convinced it was, he'd put a lot of effort into this little Christmas miracle. In his final months before getting really sick, he'd spent a considerable amount of time tying up loose ends, making sure everything was ready for the day he left them. She'd hated the preparation for doomsday, and she'd often tried to sway him to stop. But he didn't want to leave her with it all. So she'd asked that he do it when she wasn't around, the ache that it caused too much for her to bear. She'd wanted her last moments with him to build lasting memories she could hold onto. Little did she know, he'd probably been planning through this year just to be sure she'd be okay. She'd take this time at the cabin to honor him. Even in death, he was putting her first.

She went into her bedroom and got her new journal, opening it to a clean page. The journal was starting to feel like a line to Toby, a place outside of reality where the two could meet. The blank page, her thoughts, and her moving pen allowed her to access him in ways she no longer could in the regular world.

Hey Toby. I'm struggling at the moment, but not in the way you might have guessed. I know you'd never require I ask for permission to move on with life, but even still, you gave it to me. And your Christmas notes have helped me to see how much you want me to do that...

Out of nowhere, a tear slipped down her cheek. She let it fall.

You've gotten me out of the house, into a world where my past is intertwined with reality. But by following your notes, I've met someone. His name is Nick Monroe. Our meeting hit me like a flash, blind-siding me. I never saw it coming. One day I was overwhelmed by the loss of our life and the next minute, I was hoping Nick would call. I'm plagued with a strange mixture of guilt and anticipation. The thing is, if you were still here, I'd be snuggled up next to you without a care in the world. But now that you're gone, I have to see what's next, you know? Happiness is a two-edged sword sometimes.

She wiped her tears and shut the journal.

Holding her breath, she got her phone and opened the text she'd sent to Nick. Still nothing. Did she have the wrong number or something? She'd double-checked it when he gave it to her. Was he ghosting her? She went back through her wonderful memories with him and couldn't imagine he would. Maybe she'd have to make the first move. Before she could change her mind or overthink it, she fired off another message to him.

> Hey Nick! I hope you got home okay. I was wondering what you were doing over Christmas. Call me.

The answer to her internal questions could come through his response. She was sure he'd quickly respond now. She'd sent two texts, so it was definitely his turn.

She set her phone with the open screen on the table. No dots to alert her he was replying. Maybe he was one of those people who never kept his phone near him. After all, she'd hardly seen him with it the entire time they were together. Her screen eventually went dark.

It had been a long day. Time to get some sleep. She could wake up to the thrill of his response in the morning.

Chapter Eighteen

To Heather's utter disappointment, early the next morning, Nick still hadn't texted. Her mind raced with reasons he hadn't even acknowledged her. They'd had such a nice time all weekend... She inwardly scrambled for some inkling that he hadn't been sincere, but she couldn't find anything. Was there some sort of family emergency? Had something happened to him or Ophelia? She hoped he was okay. Had he lost his phone? If so, he wouldn't have her number...

Should she try to call him? No, certainly not. If he had the phone, he'd have received her texts, and—it had not even been two days—she'd look desperate or clingy. Maybe she was.

But no matter what might be going on, after the weekend they'd had together, wouldn't he have wanted to reach out to let her know why he couldn't respond? It didn't seem like him to just leave her hanging.

She tried to rationalize his behavior. *It is Christmas. Maybe he's traveling or with family, running through airports with spotty Wi-Fi.* She wanted to believe anything other than the fact that he was receiving her texts and purposely not responding.

Needing a distraction, she opened her laptop and searched for Wears Valley to see what was going on during the holidays. She and Toby hadn't ever been there over Christmas, so taking part in their festivities would be a nice diversion. She opened the first article.

Escape into an old-fashioned Christmas! In Wears Valley, Tennessee, Christmas unfolds like an old story humming through the mountains. Snow powders the edges of wooden cabins, while wreaths of cedar and holly adorn doors that have seen generations come and go.

After our famous mountain-Christmas-tree tour, featuring decorated trees, take a hayride or jump in a horse-drawn wagon and delight in the chorus of carolers in town. When you get cold, you can get hot cocoa at The Local Mug and then snuggle up in Mason's Bookshop where history buffs tell stories about Christmases past.

For those looking for a quiet retreat, bundle up in a blanket on your cabin's porch by the fire and relish the view of the distant hollows and the glitter of twinkle lights…

Wow. This might be just what she needed. She'd pack her things, stop by The Steaming Quill, get herself a decadent coffee, then crank up Christmas music and make the three-plus-hour drive to the cabin. Once she got there, she'd buy herself a few groceries and settle in for the holiday. And seeing the renovations firsthand would be a good idea since she hadn't gotten up there like she and Toby had planned.

As she folded her fuzziest sweaters, excitement built. Just as Toby's note had said, she needed to relax. She'd have sweeping views of the mountains, light a fire, and spend her first Christmas alone getting to know this new version of herself.

It didn't take her long to get her things together. She had her clothes, her new journal, a couple of novels she wanted to read, and her favorite slippers. She'd even considered packing her tree and taking it with her, but there was no way it would fit in her little car. Perhaps she could find a small one to decorate when she got there.

When Heather got to The Steaming Quill, she couldn't help but scan the tables to see if Nick would appear like magic, since it was closer to his neck of the woods—as if sheer will could summon him. But no familiar face appeared. Her fingers drummed lightly on the counter while she waited for her to-go cup, and she glanced at the door when it opened, imagining it swinging wide to reveal that easy smile. She actually missed him.

This time away would be good for her. She needed to feel strong on her own. Maybe when she got back, she'd have had some revelation about who she was and what she wanted in life, and then Nick would materialize with some grand story about why he hadn't been able to call. She pushed the growing concern out of her mind that he might be ignoring her texts. Her fragile heart couldn't take that kind of rejection.

When her name was called for the coffee, she took the cup and climbed back into her car for the long drive into the mountains. Without looking back, she took off down the road.

❄

Three and a half hours later, she found herself on the final stretch—a steep, winding road up the mountain. Her car groaned against the icy surface, and she gripped the steering wheel with both hands. She probably should have stopped in town to get groceries first. She'd assumed she could run back out, but given the weather and the treacherous roads, she now considered whether that had been a good idea. Could she get food delivery way up here? She'd never tried, since Toby had always had the cooking under control.

The narrow road was barely wide enough for two cars, so when another vehicle came toward her, she tightened her shoulders as if that would keep them on their respective sides of the road. It got closer, and suddenly, a thought hit her.

It's a white SUV.

The vehicle passed and she craned her neck to see who was driving, but the tinted windows revealed only a shadow. She glanced at the vehicle in the rearview mirror. It was a Suburban. Had the one they'd followed at the tree lot been a Suburban? This one could've been anyone, right? Except not many cabins were off this road.

The dense forest finally gave way, and she gasped. At the very top of the mountain, the cabin stood like a guard against the gray winter sky. The front yard gleamed with the glow of a single Christmas tree, every branch twinkling with tiny lights that flickered like stars. Snow cradled the roof and pooled around the porch, reflecting the warm colors of the decorations and making the tree's glow seem almost magical. From the windows, a faint golden light spilled outward, hinting at warmth inside, as if it were waiting for her to come home. Surely, holiday decorating wasn't included in the renovations...

She parked her car and put on her emergency brake and then took her bags up to the front door. With a quick slip of the key into the lock, she was inside, where she found another huge surprise. The whole interior had also been decorated for the holiday. Twinkling lights traced the edges of the room, reflecting off ornaments that hung from a tall Christmas tree in the corner, while garlands of evergreen and red berries wound along the mantel and the iron staircase that led to an upstairs loft with a view of the living room.

She shut the door behind her and walked over to the roaring fire. Someone had prepared the cabin for her. She fiddled with the stockings that swayed gently above the fireplace, each one stuffed with little surprises. She peered inside —chocolates, candy canes, candles, bubble bath... The fire crackled in the stone hearth, sending shadows dancing across the log walls. The Christmas tree in the corner was full of mountain-themed ornaments—reindeer, black bears with little red-plaid bows around their necks, miniature hot cocoa mugs, and campfire replicas. She hadn't chosen these, but they were perfect. Everywhere she looked, the cabin felt alive with peaceful joy—the kind that made time slow, inviting her to sit, breathe, and savor the moment.

With a sense of calm, she walked into the kitchen and opened the pantry, only to be surprised once more. The whole place was stocked with food, baking items, and anything she might need. A wave of relief overtook her. She wouldn't have to go out again, thank goodness. She checked the fridge: milk, orange juice, coffee cream, fruit, vegetables, condiments... champagne. She opened the freezer: frozen pizzas. She laughed. She'd told Toby more than once that frozen pizza was the closest she'd ever get to cooking anything.

The white SUV came to mind. A punch of amusement hit her when the thought arose: *Would Toby have an SUV in heaven?* It was white after all... Whoever the angel was who'd done this for her, they'd thought of everything.

Under the tree were three wrapped gifts. What could they be? She wouldn't rush to open them. It was Christmas Eve. She could at least wait for tomorrow.

She found a radio in the kitchen and tuned it to Christmas music, the familiar songs winding through the house as she carried her bags up the stairs to the master bedroom. She unpacked, piling her heavy sweaters into the deep dresser drawers. The bedspread she'd chosen was quilted with various patterns on each square, and across from the bed, in the fireplace, a fire was going already.

She looked around at the evidence of someone having been there. A twinge of worry overtook her as Marion's warnings came back. Was the SUV the same one they'd seen at the tree lot? To do all this, someone else had to have a key to the cabin, but she'd locked the extra security latch on the doors when she'd come inside, so no one could get in. And with all her provisions, she wouldn't have to go outside again until she was ready to go back home. She'd be fine.

Just to be extra safe, she clutched her phone and walked around to every room, checking behind shower curtains, under beds, in closets, until she'd exhausted every possible hiding spot. No one was there.

With everything unpacked, she took one of her novels downstairs and preheated the oven to bake one of the frozen pizzas. Then she took down a stocking and dumped it on the coffee table, picking through the contents and selecting a few of her favorite chocolates—hazelnut, ganache, and coconut cream. While the oven preheated, she curled up in the armchair by the fire, a blanket she'd gotten from a basket on the hearth draped over her knees as the soft hum of the radio filled the cabin with holiday tunes. The DJ's voice threaded through the music, and it felt as though someone was sitting across from her, sharing a laugh or a quiet sigh. Snow pressed against the windows in gentle drifts, but inside, the crackle of the fire and the DJ's smooth cadence made the cabin feel less lonely, as if the world beyond the mountains had completely disappeared. As the music played, she opened her book, a small, comforting reminder that even in solitude, she wasn't entirely alone.

Her phone rang on the table, interrupting her little moment.

Hopeful the caller might be Nick, she jumped up and ran over to answer.

Marion.

"How was the drive?" Marion asked.

"Snowy. I'd originally thought I'd do some things in town, but Toby always used to drive, and I'm not comfortable going up and down the mountain." With the phone on speaker, she went into the kitchen and turned down the radio.

"Do you feel safe out there by yourself?"

"You'd be proud of me. I checked the entire house to be sure it's empty, and I locked the extra locks on all the doors, so no one can get in." She walked back into the living room and pulled the latch on the sliding doors that opened to the deck, then walked out into the cold. "And the only door that matters is the front door, because out back it's gotta be a couple hundred feet down. I'm outside looking at it now."

"What's the view like?" Marion asked.

"Snowcapped mountains as far as I can see, and at the bottom is a lake. The edges are frozen, and they sparkle when the sun peeks through the clouds."

"Definitely worth staying put. And staying in will give you lots of reading time. Did you bring some of the books we bought?"

"I did. And there's bubble bath." She went back inside and closed the door behind her, going to the fire and standing in front of the popping flames with a shiver.

"How is the cabin?"

"It's gorgeous. It was decorated for Christmas and stocked with food. I've got chocolate, hot cocoa, and champagne. There were even fires going when I got here." The oven had preheated, so she left the fire and slid the pizza in.

"Wow."

"It'll be nice to have a couple days to myself. In Greenville, Nick and I spent a lot of time together, but here, I can relax."

"Has Nick called?"

She chewed her lip. "Not yet. But I texted him again, so now the ball is really in his court."

"I'm sure he will eventually. Guys often operate on a different schedule than we do." She giggled down the line, but Heather still wondered about Nick's silence. "Well, enjoy the time alone. Call me when you get bored."

"I will."

She hung up the phone and decided that right now was as good a time as any to break into the champagne. She pulled a flute from the cabinet. Then she took the bottle from the fridge, untwisted the metal tab on the wire cage that protected the cork, covered it with a towel, and popped it open. It fizzed as she poured it into the glass. With a wedge of the cork back into the bottle and a refold of the towel, she cleaned up.

Now, back to those chocolates...

❄

As Heather sat at the rustic family-sized table in the kitchen, with a view of the mountains out back, she considered how Toby's family had gathered there in generations past. She nibbled her pizza, imagining every seat full, arms passing large bowls of mashed potatoes and platters of turkey while Christmas music played low on the radio like it was at that moment.

Who had decorated for her and transformed this cabin into the gorgeous retreat she was enjoying now? And was someone in a white SUV delivering all this to her? She tried to place which one of Toby's friends would have taken on this massive endeavor. While there were people who would do things for him, running all these notes around and preparing a cabin wasn't an easy ask. And like she'd told her mom, she didn't know anyone with a white SUV. Maybe after Christmas, they'd reveal themselves and the mystery would be solved. Then she could invite them to use the cabin as a thank-you. If she couldn't fill it with family, she could fill it with friends.

Over the last year, she hadn't even considered what she'd do with this place. Even visiting hadn't crossed her mind. She'd been paralyzed by her grief and so worried by reporters that she hadn't given her sanity much attention. Before that, she'd been consumed with Toby's health, brushing up on her degree, and getting a job—to appease Toby, really; not for herself.

All the while, this gem had been waiting for her.

Even though they'd renovated, it didn't have Toby's touch. Had he been given enough time to get in there, he'd have hung his prized guitars down the wall next to the view in the living room or framed sheet music to put in the hallway upstairs. But he'd left her to take care of those things.

In the quiet of late afternoon, it seemed to call out to her to fill it with a family—the one thing she couldn't do. What would the patter of tiny feet sound like against these floors? What would the Christmas tree look like surrounded by sleepy-eyed children in pajamas, still recovering from all the wonderful holiday events downtown, all clamoring to see which presents were theirs?

Only then, through the pain that rose, causing a thickness in her chest, did she realize that Toby's "Christmas With You" was playing on the radio. She closed her eyes and focused on the lyrics:

If I could ever make that call
If the world allowed me to break the wall
I'd run to you, rush to you

If I could do it at all
And tell you that I'd spend
Christmas with you...

While she'd always known the lyrics had been about a woman that a man loved from afar and could never have, today, they felt like a direct message straight to her from heaven. As the rest of the song played, tears streamed from her eyes.

Oh, Toby, why have you done all this?

While she could guess that it was his way of planning one last Christmas, her question was more about how much it made her miss him. She was still straddling her old life with Toby and her new one without him, wondering if she'd ever break free from the chasm.

Chapter Nineteen

It was Christmas morning and, surprisingly, Heather had slept until after nine. It had been a long time since she'd stayed in bed that long. Even though she'd slept really deeply, a part of her remembered feeling during the night as if she were closer to Toby. Perhaps that was why she felt so rested this morning.

And she'd nearly made it through the holiday—stronger than she'd imagined she'd be, but still dealing with the haunting loss of her old life and the man she loved. She had to admit that all the notes had helped her through the season. Before them, she'd been binging her wedding video and sobbing into balled-up tissues. But as Toby had suggested, she got out, pushed herself into the world on a personal level, rather than just going to work, and she'd even met someone who had given her hope.

Although Nick still hadn't called or texted. And by this point, it seemed he wasn't going to. Had he panicked and changed his mind about her? Had she somehow come on too strong? Perhaps she shouldn't have shared anything personal with him. Had she crossed some kind of early dating line? She didn't know how to date anymore, and she didn't want to play games. After all she'd shared with Nick, he could at least have had the decency to respond to her.

But it was the holiday, and he did have a life outside of his phone. It still didn't make his silence right. And she couldn't really explain away his behavior. But now wasn't the time to ponder it.

There was something about Christmas morning that lifted her mood. It didn't matter that she was by herself or still figuring out her life. This morning always brought with it a kind of hope that she couldn't harness at any other time of the year.

Her thick, woolly socks and fluffy bathrobe kept her warm as she padded downstairs to throw a couple more logs into the fireplace to heat up the living area for the day. She lit the fire with a match from a dish next to the pile of kindling on the hearth and warmed her hands.

After a few poker stokes of the fire to really get it going, she went into the kitchen and made some coffee. The hearty aroma filled the air, giving the morning a nostalgic feel. Growing up, that scent had been present all the Christmases she'd come running down the stairs to unwrap presents.

Regardless of whether she'd ever get to the bottom of Nick's silence, after a good cry and a sound night's sleep, this Christmas might feel less like a gap between her two lives and instead more like a bookend. While Toby might have planned these letters, certainly, he hadn't planned them to continue forever, and this holiday would probably be his final goodbye, which was bittersweet. His notes had been enough to get her through and, in a strange way, they'd helped her see that when she was ready, she could step into her future. While she wasn't entirely healed, she'd proven to herself she could manage.

The coffee finished brewing, so she made herself a cup with cream and sugar and took it into the living room, stopping to admire the view through the sliding glass doors. A cardinal rested on a nearby branch, its red coloring standing out against the gray sky. The view of the rounded mountains, the snow piled on the branches of the trees, and the ripples on the lake below, made her feel cocooned from the world.

She sat next to the fire and opened her novel, losing herself in the story and letting go of time for a little while. The morning stretched on while she settled into the comfort of her surroundings, warmed by the fire.

Pages and pages later, after she'd finally gotten up to make herself some breakfast and a second cup of coffee, she faced the tree. It was still lit. She hadn't had the heart to turn it off when she went to bed. The warm golden lights had made her feel less alone.

Underneath sat the three presents, wrapped in white paper with red bows. There was a time not long ago when she would've crumbled at the thought of receiving surprise presents from Toby, but now she felt an incredible bond with him because of his gifts. While she still missed him and mourned the future they wouldn't have together, it was as if they were still in this thing called life by each other's side, just in a form they didn't expect. She was actually itching to know what he could've possibly dreamed up to give her this day.

Heather sat cross-legged on the floor, set down her coffee beside her, and reached in for the first gift. Slowly, she untied the ribbon. Then she slipped her finger under the tape on one end, pulling the paper loose. She ripped the rest, revealing a box with no logos or printing of any kind. When she shimmied off the lid, inside was a folder and another red-and-white envelope. She opened the note and began to read.

This folder holds new songs you've never

heard before. I thought about sharing it with you while I was sick, but figured I'd hold out and do it in the grandest way I could think of. They're entirely yours now. I sent this to my publisher as well, so they've got them. I already fulfilled my contract, but I know they're interested if you want to release more of my music. Do whatever you want with them, with my blessing.

Merry Christmas.

With tears in her eyes, she thumbed through the handwritten sheets of notebook paper, none of them familiar: "Into the Night," "That Thing You Do," "Highway 40," "The Happy One," "The Place I Call Home," "If You Don't"... His music was his entire world, and he kept a lot of his songs under wraps until he was done with them, so by reading these words, she was able to get a little more of *him*—the version of Toby who strummed for hours on the sofa, scratching down phrases and ideas. This Christmas, he'd managed to give her his heart—all of him.

Above the lyrics, he'd penciled in music notes. She not only had the words, but if she could get someone to read the notes and play them for her, she had the tune as well. Not to mention she had an entire album's worth, maybe more. While Toby couldn't cut another album, his talent might be able to live on in other artists.

She held the folder to her chest. *Incredible.*

Taking her time, she leafed through the pages and sipped her coffee. Surrounded by the rustic cabin and roaring fire, she felt that Christmas hope grow a little bigger.

Thank you for all this, Toby. She sent the thought into the air, blinking away tears, her heart full.

She gazed at the other presents. Toby had already given her enough. What else could she possibly get to top this?

She opened the second gift—a binder and another note. Before looking inside the binder, she read his letter.

> In a way, all this was for me too, because I got to plan one more Christmas for you. Seeing you light up was worth all the planning every year. But this time, I'll need your help. This notebook has all my recipes in it—the ones I used to make for Christmas. The meatloaf is, of course, included...

She laughed, more tears welling up, her heart so full it felt as if it would burst. She finished the letter.

> I've stocked the cabin with the supplies you need to make whatever you want to bake from these recipes. Choose your favorites. I'll be right there beside you.

She put her hands over her lips, tears now streaming down her cheeks. All she had left to open was the final gift, and she couldn't help but feel it could be Toby's last message to her.

Wanting to stretch the moment, she decided to leave it where it was.

She took the recipes and her mug of coffee into the kitchen and opened to the first page.

Toby's Sugar Cookies
As Sweet As Heather

She turned on the radio and gathered the supplies she'd need for the first recipe. The cabin was equipped with measuring spoons and cups, baking dishes, large bowls, a mixer... No detail had been missed.

While preheating the oven, Marion called, so she put the phone on speaker and turned down the radio.

"Merry Christmas," she said, unwrapping a stick of butter.

"Merry Christmas! How was your night?"

"Good. I slept like a baby, tucked up here in the mountains. How about you? How are you and Anthony doing?"

"We had a conversation last night, actually. While we sat on our sofa reading, I mentioned that it had crossed my mind how much fun it would be to spend Christmas Eve focused on the magic of the season for a little one."

Heather sighed as she put the butter in the microwave to soften it, her own thought about family surfacing again. "That was brave to bring it up. What did he say?"

"I expected an intense debate, but he was calm, and for the first time since the mention of kids, he explained himself. He told me that he was afraid."

"Afraid? Of what?" Heather pulled a bowl out of the cabinet and added the butter.

"He didn't have the best upbringing, and he worries he'll fail as a father. He works all the time, and he wants to be able to devote himself to the law firm without feeling guilty."

Heather got out the sugar. "I applaud his honesty. That gives you a starting point in therapy."

"From what he's told me about his childhood, he definitely wasn't the center of his father's world, and I think he both understands the need to work and provide for his family, and his childhood desire to have a father who could take him under his wing."

"Those are valid feelings," Heather said, dumping a measuring cup of sugar over the butter and combining the two.

"It's a start, for sure," Marion said. "How about you? Any new developments with the notes or Toby?"

"I've been able to do a lot of thinking, and I've had some closure. And I got presents this time."

"Really? Do tell!"

As she measured flour and dumped it into the bowl, she told Marion all about the notes, the songs, and the recipes. "I have one more gift to open, but I saved it. I'm actually making sugar cookies right now, although they don't look as fluffy as Toby's used to."

"Oh, I love that so much. When are you saving the last one for?"

Heather wiped her hands on the dish towel. "I'm not sure. Maybe I just want to hang onto it because I waffle between wanting to move forward and not letting go. How was *your* Christmas morning? Get any long-awaited gifts?"

"It was wonderful. We tore through our presents, and then I made breakfast. Anthony got me a new leather coat."

"Fancy. Did Scarlett get anything?"

"Of course. She got a sweater that she hates and a climbing tower. Now she's staring at me while I sit here. Anthony's putting together his new weight bench I got him."

Heather laughed. "Well, if you get too bored, I'm only three hours away."

"Don't tempt me."

"Bring Anthony and Scarlett. But I'd take Anthony's truck. The drive up here is snowy..."

"Good to know. Thanks for the invite. I'll keep you posted if we change plans."

"Seriously. It's just me here. I'd love the company, and I could show you all the renovations."

While she understood that it was the holidays, Heather would love nothing more than to share the cabin with people she cared about. If not now, she'd definitely make this a place to gather from here on out.

Chapter Twenty

By early afternoon, Heather had made both sugar and gingerbread cookies as well as Toby's famous marshmallow fudge. While the treats cooled, she'd had a bubble bath and treated herself to another glass of champagne. Now, dressed in a fresh set of clothes and feeling merry as snow fell lightly outside like feathers, she pulled out her journal and took it to the sofa. Curling up with the leather book in her lap, she started to write.

Toby, you've blown me away with all this. It's amazing how you were able to whip me up into this whirlwind with your messages. I began this journal thinking it would be my love letter to you, but in true Toby form, you've outdone me on the creative front, and your letters are larger than life (pun intended?). In fact, I'm surprised by your incredibly clear message that I need to get out more. Which is interesting, given that you were always the one who skirted around the public. While I enjoyed being out and about, I loved your quiet nature. That's probably why, instead of this journal being a love letter, my entries have been more of a conversation with you, talking through my thoughts. You were the best listener. So I'm going to keep this journal as a place where I can talk to you. Thanks in advance for listening.

Heather closed the journal, set it on the table, and decided to try her hand at one of Toby's other recipes: her favorite, the meatloaf casserole. She got up and went into the kitchen.

Working beside the warmth of the preheating oven, she placed bread slices in the bottom of an oiled baking dish, humming along to the radio. She was noticeably fine alone in the cabin, preparing her meal. While she'd love to have a big family running around, she could do this too. Best of all, a tiny spark of optimism had emerged with her decision that her solitary life might not last forever, so she could relax into the tasks for the season that she was in.

She still couldn't get over how much her perspective had changed in such a short time. And, if she were being honest with herself, it was due to Toby *and* Nick. Without Toby's notes, she'd have never met Nick. And without Nick, she'd have had a much harder time finding promise in her future. She'd needed both Toby and Nick, which confused her. Toby reaching out one last time made sense, given who he was, but Nick's silence didn't. And if things were meant to happen, and she'd been meant to meet Nick, how could it all end in silence?

Her next season might look quite different if Nick never responded. She'd been pushing the idea that he was ignoring her texts out of her mind, but as time went on, she was starting to worry. Especially after having texted him again. The rationalization that maybe he was giving her space over the holiday to enjoy her family and friends had dwindled, especially in light of the fact that she'd broken that silence with another message.

His complete disregard for her texts had her wondering if she even knew him at all. He'd made her feel so special, and his abrupt abandonment had knocked her to her knees. She'd even told him about Toby—a subject she never broached with anyone. Wouldn't he have been decent enough to check on her over the holiday? Perhaps that was why Toby had kept things to himself. Maybe he knew enough about people to foresee these kinds of things when she didn't.

Continuing to question the situation, she washed her hands and checked her phone, opening the text chain with Nick. Still only her two unanswered text bubbles. Then her phone went off in her hand, startling her, and she dropped the device onto the hardwood floor. Her heart pounding, she picked it up and answered.

"Hey!" Marion's chipper voice came through the phone.

"Hi."

"You okay? You sound flustered."

"Oh, I dropped the phone. I'm just cooking meatloaf casserole for lunch."

"Isn't that your favorite?"

"One of them."

"Will there be enough for three?"

Heather perked up. "Are you thinking of coming?"

"Anthony has had it with weight-bench construction. He wants to watch football and relax. I told him I know the perfect place."

Heather burst into a smile, unable to quiet her squeal. "When can you get here?"

"We're all packed and can be there by dinnertime."

"I'll text you the location. Be careful! It's starting to snow again."

"Oh, I can't wait! Need me to bring anything?" Marion asked.

"I've got enough food to feed an army. If you want a specific wine or something, you can bring that. I've got champagne, and coffee for the morning."

Marion let out a loud "Ha!" and said, "I've already packed wine and Anthony's beers!"

"I should've guessed."

"Okay! I'll see you soon. Love you!"

"Be careful!" she said again.

When they got off the call, she texted Marion directions, set her phone on the table, and went back into the kitchen, glad for the distraction from Nick.

❄

About four hours later, with the fire going and the candles lit, the sound of tires grinding on the snow outside pulled Heather to the window. Anthony's truck came to a stop next to the outdoor Christmas tree, and Marion hopped out of the passenger seat, holding Scarlett's carrier.

With exuberant excitement, Heather unlatched the front door and swung it open. Anthony waved before ducking behind his seat in the truck and retrieving a suitcase, a few bags, and a small cooler, while Marion jogged through the snow with her free arm outstretched.

"We made it!" She threw her arm around Heather and gave her a squeeze, the carrier by her side.

Her best friend's embrace was the best feeling.

"I waited to bake the casserole for dinner," Heather said, rubbing Scarlett's little head through the small grate, "so it's almost done. I hope you're hungry."

"I'm definitely hungry," Anthony said, stepping up next to them, loaded down with bags. He kicked the snow off his shoes. "Hey, Heather. Good to see you." He leaned in and gave her a side hug.

"Same." She ushered them inside the warm cabin and closed the door.

Marion gazed around the open living room and kitchen. "This place is gorgeous, Heather." She ran her hand along the butcher-block island Toby had kept from the original layout and had refinished.

"Thank you," Heather said, wishing Toby could have enjoyed the fruits of all his planning.

"I don't like showing up empty-handed," Anthony said. "I'd have brought steaks or something, but Marion insisted you told her that food was plenty and you didn't need anything else."

"I have more than enough to sustain us," she said.

Marion dropped her bag, took Scarlett out of the carrier and cradled the little kitten. "Oh wow, this is incredible," she said, looking around.

"I'm tickled with the renovations." Heather picked up the TV remote and flicked through the stations until she found football for Anthony. "Let me help you with your things."

Anthony waved her off. "No, no. You two enjoy yourselves. Just tell me where to go." He slung Marion's bags over his arm and picked up the suitcase.

"Your room's the second door on the left upstairs. Let me know if you need anything."

"Okay." He adjusted the bags once more. "Be right back. Marion, you want to unpack the cooler?"

"Unpack the wine and beer? Silly question." Marion winked at Heather and handed Scarlett to her.

While Marion toted the cooler into the kitchen, Heather followed, holding the purring ball of fur. She clicked on the radio, turning the volume low so they could still carry on a conversation.

"She loves to be held, so she's easy to travel with."

Heather stroked the kitten's soft head.

Marion set the cooler on the counter and unzipped it. "It smells so good in here."

"I've been cooking all day." Heather gestured toward the dining table that now held Christmas platters of cookies. "Help yourself."

Wide-eyed, Marion abandoned the cooler and moved to the table, selecting a gingerbread cookie and taking a nibble. "Look at you, the little domestic goddess."

"I was inspired."

Marion grinned at her, clearly delighted to see her happy. Then she sobered and leaned in. "Thank you for having us," she whispered. "I think the time away from our regular lives might give us a chance to talk with no distractions." She nodded in the direction of the empty stairway.

"I hope so," Heather said with an air of optimism.

"Got any wine glasses?"

"Yep. How many do we need?" She handed the kitten back to Marion.

"Two if you want a glass. Anthony packed his beer so doesn't need any, but I brought us girls rosé." She began loading beverages into the fridge.

"Definitely two then."

Heather retrieved the glasses while Marion unzipped the side of the cooler and retrieved a corkscrew. Marion set Scarlett down to uncork the wine. The kitten purred and rubbed against her leg.

Just then, the timer went off, so Heather slipped on the oven mitts and pulled out the casserole, sending a savory aroma into the air that she hadn't smelled in so long. She set the steaming, bubbling dish on a trivet.

"Holy smokes, that looks divine. Let me get Scarlett's food ready so she doesn't decide to help herself."

Marion handed Heather a glass of wine and then unpacked two small bowls, filling one with tap water and another with kibble.

Lost in nostalgia, Heather located a serving spoon and sank it into the cheesy dish.

"How many nights in a row could you eat this?" she'd asked Toby, draping her arms around him while he dished her a plate.

He twisted around and kissed her nose. "Maybe two nights a week?"

"Only two?" she playfully whined.

"You can't live on meatloaf casserole."

"Why not? It's got a few veggies in there, protein, healthy fats..."

He laughed, his eyes closing the way they did when he shook his head at her, amused.

Marion set the kitten's bowls against the wall on the other side of the table. Scarlett followed her, lapping the water before jumping up to the windowsill, where she perched to take in the view.

"She's such a gorgeous little thing," Heather said before sipping her wine, relishing the crisp sweetness of it to get the old memory out of her mind. "I'm glad you could bring her."

"She's really easygoing. She'll probably hang out in that window until we sit down in the living room. Then she'll want to curl up in one of our laps." Marion eyed Heather. "You okay?"

Heather took in a breath. "I'm fine. I just realized I haven't had Toby's casserole in over a year. He couldn't make it when he was sick, and I didn't have the recipe until now."

"It's awesome that you have it," Marion said. "He thought of everything, didn't he?"

Heather swallowed back her emotion. "Yeah. Once, I'd

considered calling his great-aunt Nancy to ask for it. He'd mentioned it was hers to begin with. But I could never bring myself to because she'd want to talk about Toby, and it's been tough to have a light conversation about him."

"You're doing great right now," Marion pointed out.

"Thanks." Wanting a diversion so she wouldn't get too lost in her feelings, she changed gears. "With the game on, I'm thinking we'll be in the living room sooner rather than later. Want to eat dinner in there?"

"I'm up for that," Anthony said, coming down the stairs and into the kitchen. "I've got everything unpacked except this." He held up a small bag of litter and a travel-sized litter box. "Where should I set it up?"

"There's a mudroom just down the hall." Heather pointed past him. "Think she'll look for it?"

"She's smart. She'll be able to find it." Marion took a bottle of beer out of the fridge and held it out to Anthony. "Thank you for unpacking." She smiled at him, a depth in her gaze that Heather hadn't ever seen. Maybe this would be good for them.

He took the bottle from her, kissed her cheek, and then carried the litterbox down the hall.

As she dished out their dinner, Heather's heart was full. Toby just might have given her the best Christmas he could have, apart from him being there with them.

Chapter Twenty-One

"I'm out." Anthony laid his last playing card on the run of diamonds beside his empty beer bottles as the TV announcers chattered on in the other room.

Marion and Heather simultaneously threw up their hands.

"Noooo!" Marion called. "I had one more card, and it would've fit right there." She tapped another run.

"I won again." With a swipe of his hand, Anthony gathered the cards and piled them into a deck, cutting it and shuffling them.

"Best out of five!" Marion called.

Anthony threw his head back with a laugh and set the deck on the table. "We've done best out of three and now four. I still won. We've been playing cards for two hours. And I want to take a break and eat more of Heather's cookies." He grabbed a sugar cookie and a fudge square, pushed back from the table, and kissed Marion on the top of her head. "The game's coming on. It's the Broncos and the Chiefs—we won't want to miss it."

With a dramatic but lighthearted sigh, Marion scooped up Scarlett and gathered their glasses and bottles, setting them one by one beside the sink while Heather filled a small plate of treats. They'd had a full evening after dinner, alternating between chatting and playing various card games with the deck Marion had wisely brought. Their light banter had kept Heather from pondering what would happen after the holiday. A few days ago, she'd have thought it might include Nick, but now she wasn't so sure. That disappointment was a weight she knew she'd have to bear once she was alone again. But tonight, the sound of chatter and laughter, along with the buzz of the football game, offered a sense of normalcy she hadn't felt in a long time.

"That was a blast." Marion pinched a couple more sugar cookies and added them to the plate. "Now," she said pointedly, "the night could turn, depending on the competence of the Broncos..." She nodded toward the living-room TV. "We'd better make some hot cocoa to manage the stress of it. We can suffer through anything with marshmallows and peppermint."

Heather nodded with mock seriousness.

A few minutes later, bringing a plate of cookies, a bowl of popcorn, and two hot chocolates with whipped cream and peppermint sprinkles into the living room, Marion and Heather, along with Scarlett, joined Anthony on the sofa. As the snow gently fell against a dark sky, dusting the Adirondack chairs outside, they settled in for a night of football. To Anthony's joy, and Marion's relief, the Broncos beat the Chiefs by one touchdown.

After the game, as they sat among the empty plates and cups, Marion looked over at the tree. "What do you think that present is under there?" She pointed to the final white gift with the red bow.

"Whatever it is, I'm thinking it's the last thing I'll get from Toby."

Anthony clicked off the TV. "Christmas is almost over. When are you planning to open it?"

Heather hesitated.

Marion repositioned Scarlett in her lap. "What's wrong?"

Heather stared at the gift, taking a few long, slow breaths to steady herself. "There was a time in all this when I was so ready to move on that I wanted the gifts to stop. But it wasn't until I made this trip that I really got to process the full breadth of what Toby has accomplished for me. While my future still isn't planned out with a nice, neat bow like that gift, I know I can handle it better after hearing from him. In a way, having him with me this Christmas makes me feel like he's always there." Her voice broke on the final word, tears welling in her eyes. She cleared her throat. "Sorry."

Marion handed Scarlett to Anthony. "Don't be sorry. We're here for you."

"I should open the final gift," Heather said, still trying to convince herself to do it.

Marion put her arm around her and gave her a squeeze. "Only if you want to."

"Like Anthony said, Christmas is almost over. There's no better time to do it than now, when I'm with you two and we've had such a wonderful, memorable day." Heather gently pulled out of Marion's embrace, reached down, and took Toby's final gift from under the tree. "All good things come to an end, and it's best that I face this final moment while I have you here to support me."

Marion placed a hand on her back. "Whenever you're ready."

Heather set the present in her lap, gently untied the ribbon, and loosened the tape, the paper falling around the box. She slipped her fingers under the edge and lifted the lid. Beneath a mass of tissue paper, she pulled out a photo album. Peeking out from the back of the album was another red-and-white envelope.

Still not fully prepared to read his final message to her, she opened the album cover, and immediately tears overflowed. She ran her fingers over the first photo—her favorite, taken two years ago, at the holiday gala for Stargate Publishing. He looked so handsome and full of life in his tuxedo, and she hung on his arm in that red dress that had driven him crazy, smiling innocently.

Her lip wobbled. "I was looking for this photo a while ago." She cleared her throat again, unable to keep her jagged breaths manageable. Toby'd had it all under control, just like he'd told her.

Anthony got up and returned with a box of tissues from the bathroom.

"Thank you," she said, through the blur of tears. "I can look at this later. I don't want to bring you both down." She sniffled, snatching a tissue from the box.

"No, no," Marion said, ever the supportive friend.

"I'll set up Scarlett's bed area and take her litter box upstairs," Anthony said, his look letting them know he was giving them a chance to be together without an extra set of eyes.

Marion handed him the kitten. "Thanks."

"No problem."

When it was just the two women, Marion leaned in. "Tell me about the photos."

With a deep breath, Heather tapped the second photo on the page. "This one was taken on our first date. He took me bowling, and I got my fingers stuck in the ball," she said with a half whimper and half laugh. "We tried everything—soap and water, hand lotion, you name it. He ran down the street to the gas station to see if they had any other ideas and came back with a bottle of tanning lotion. It worked, but I smelled like coconuts for the rest of the night." She shook her head. "We could only go up from there."

Marion grinned. "I've never heard that story."

"I've never told it to anyone." It felt good to share. She turned the page, revealing another wonderful memory. She was blowing out her birthday candles while Toby looked on adoringly. "We were supposed to go skiing, but at the airport the flight was canceled due to a snowstorm, so right there, he rebooked and got us a long weekend in Cancun. We jumped on the plane, both our suitcases full of sweaters and ski overalls. We bought swimsuits and lived in them. I only bought one dress to go to dinner. It was magical."

"It sounds like it."

They flipped through the rest of the photos, Heather's emotions flaring the entire time. When they got to the end, she could hardly see, and her nose was stuffy from crying. But it was a good cry. Instead of feeling his absence, she had celebrated the man he was and the couple they were together. She closed the book and put it back into the box.

Marion picked up the envelope that had slipped out while they were flipping pages and handed it to Heather. She put it under the tree, next to the box.

"Aren't you going to open it?"

She'd hang onto him one more day. "I'll do it tomorrow." That tiny prick of fear that had plagued her in his final days returned—the imminent goodbye. "He always had all the answers," she said, her voice breaking.

Marion offered an empathetic smile. "So do you. You just got used to leaning on Toby for them. But when it comes down to it, you're pretty good at finding the answers you need."

Heather gave Marion a hug and breathed in her sweet perfume, knowing she was right, but having a hard time accepting it, nonetheless. While the rest of her life wasn't quite so scary anymore, the memories were still raw.

Chapter Twenty-Two

"I was wondering, what do you think about staying another night?" Heather asked the next morning, as she sat across from Marion at the table with a cinnamon roll from a batch they'd baked to hold them over until later, when they could have a big breakfast.

Since last night, Heather had been wrestling with the idea of going back to the real world, and it would be easy to extend her stay. After all, she owned the place. "I don't really have anything to come home to." Heather wrapped her hands around her coffee mug to warm them.

"We could stay... Anthony's off work until after New Year's, and he mentioned how great it would be to spend a couple days here. And after Christmas, I'll bet there's no line for the carriage rides in town." Marion picked up her phone and pulled up the community's website. "Anthony's truck has four-wheel drive. He could take us. And if he doesn't want to go, I'm sure he'd be delighted to stay in with Scarlett and watch football all day while we spend the afternoon shopping."

"What am I doing?" he asked, coming into the kitchen holding Scarlett.

"Either shopping with us or driving us into town and hanging with Scarlett at the cabin until we need you. And we're staying another night." Marion flashed a wide smile.

"Another night in this place is going to be tough," he said sarcastically as the tree glimmered behind him. "I'd need to have some sort of compensation." He bent over the tray of hot rolls. "Mm. You can pay me in these."

"Easy." Heather got up, plated a couple of the sticky rolls, and set them on the counter.

Anthony passed the cat to Marion and washed his hands.

"There's milk in the fridge if you want some, or we have coffee," she said. "The glasses and mugs are to the right of the sink."

"Aren't we sweet, making treats and having coffee brewed as soon as your feet hit the floor?" Marion asked in a syrupy voice. "With that kind of service, I'd think you might throw in a souvenir option. Maybe later you and I could pick out some of those mineral bath salts that were in Heather's stocking. I've found the store that has them."

Anthony playfully shook his head. "Sure."

Marion brightened and leaned over to Heather, pretending to keep her whisper from Anthony. "He's a different person here. He never commits to beauty products."

He squinted at her. "Then I'll need a few gingerbread cookies later."

"Done! Heather, don't eat any more gingerbread cookies. We need them for leverage."

"If we run out of them, we can always make more. I've got enough ingredients," Heather said, egging them on, overjoyed to see them playful and happy together.

"Oooh." Marion took the bait. "Think how many bath salts I could buy with a whole batch!" She turned her phone around so Heather could view the website. "Let's make another cup of coffee and map out our plan for the day. Man the kitty." She passed Scarlett to Anthony over the table.

"I'll make us another pot," Heather said.

"I'm willing to bet that you two can absolutely handle the task of mapping out shopping, but I'll be in the living room if you need me." Anthony shifted Scarlett, pinning her between his body and forearm, put one of the cinnamon rolls between his teeth, and carried his plate, coffee, and cat into the other room. A minute or so later, the sound of sports announcers filtered into the kitchen.

Heather got up and poured them each a mug of coffee, then found a pad of paper and a pen in the drawer.

"Okay," Marion said, as Heather set a mug in front of her. "If we go out this afternoon, we can catch a carriage ride through town at two. That will take us past the bookshop." She scribbled the words "carriage," then "bookshop" on the pad of paper. "Anthony," she called. "Want to take a carriage ride at two?"

"Sure," he said over his shoulder.

"Okay." She turned to Heather. "Then, if it's not too cold, we could walk around town, maybe see the art gallery and the chapel, and then shop for a bit until four."

"That sounds wonderful."

"And *then*, if we can still feel our toes, the sun should be setting around four thirty, and we could take a hayride through the side roads for the Christmas-tree tour. Think you're up for it?"

Heather picked up her mug, excitement building. "I'm totally up for it. We can loaf around this morning, make a big breakfast, and then head out."

The day was shaping up to be an incredible one.

❄

One of the two Clydesdale horses snorted, its reins jingling.

"I think we owe Toby a huge thank-you," Marion said to Heather as Anthony helped his wife climb up the step into the ornate carriage. "Without his thoughtfulness, none of this would be possible."

They'd taken a couple of quilts from the closet in the cabin, rolled them up, and brought them to keep warm on the ride. Heather spread hers over her legs.

"I know. I still can't get over it. He could barely keep up with boxing a few documents for storage, and whenever I came home from work, he was asleep. I have no idea how he managed lining everything up and all the letters... I keep trying to figure that out."

"You always said he could do amazing things," Marion said.

"Yeah, but this would be tough for anyone, given what he was dealing with."

Marion shook her head, looking baffled as Anthony squeezed in beside her, sandwiching her in the middle.

"I still have one more envelope to open," Heather said.

"Hopefully it's not time sensitive." Marion made a face.

Heather laughed. "Yeah, I hope not too."

As the carriage lurched forward, Marion looked around. "No white SUVs in sight, so we're probably okay to wait."

"It is kind of weird to think that someone might be watching to see when we do certain things. I have to admit that this morning, lying in bed, I wondered—hoped—if it could be Nick and that's why he hasn't called. I keep waiting for him to pop out around every corner."

"He hasn't responded at all?"

"No. I keep thinking about it, and I'm sure he has a good reason. He wouldn't just ghost somebody. And in a way, the quiet time was helpful because it gave me space to get my head straight. I'd be ready for anything that happened between us. I feel strong—like I can stand on my own two feet. And I have to wonder if when I get back home, Nick will do something amazing, because a big gesture sounds like him." She thought her heart might burst with the anticipation of seeing him again.

Marion brightened. "Wouldn't that be incredible if he *was* the one behind the notes?"

"Too good to be true," Heather said, but deep down, she wished it could be him. "But I did sit next to him on the same plane. He could've been following me. As far as I know, he was in Greenville for an actual meeting, but what if he wasn't? What if he was behind all this, and he's waiting to give me time to process it all before we jump into something?"

Marion pulled her blanket over her arms. "Yeah, but if he's behind it and he was here, wouldn't he text you back to throw you off the scent?"

Heather pursed her lips in thought. "You'd think so. But the situation might also be weird for him. If all the notes really *have* been delivered by Nick, it might feel awkward to move forward with me while he's delivering Toby's messages."

Marion offered an empathetic tilt of her head. "You've got a point. Give him a little time. Maybe once you get through the holiday, he'll call."

They clip-clopped down a quiet ribbon of road framed by the Smoky Mountains that made up the main street in Wears Valley.

"The pessimistic side of me, however, worries that, if Nick isn't behind these notes, then *I'm* the reason he hasn't responded, that I ruined things."

Marion twisted toward her. "How?"

"I told him about Toby, and I also said I felt stronger after having met him. So I dropped the bomb that I'm a widow *and* I probably sounded clingy. He might have gone running for the hills. But I was just being honest." She shook her head. "I don't know how to do the dating thing."

"From a guy's perspective, I'm sure you're overthinking," Anthony said, joining the conversation.

Heather pulled the blankets up tighter, being mindful not to take too much from Anthony's end. "That makes me feel better. But am I overthinking? Because he's gone completely silent. As in not even responding to my question."

"You could try to call and ask him," Marion suggested.

"No way. Not after two ignored texts. I have my dignity." She pointed out the log cabins and small shops that sat back from the pavement, their porches dotted with rocking chairs and trimmed with evergreen garlands, red bows, and soft white lights that glowed against the gray mist in the winter air. Anthony and Marion were there to enjoy the holiday. They didn't need to get tangled in her drama.

But she couldn't let Nick's silence go, and it was nice to bat around her thoughts with them. All she wanted to do was make sense of the situation. "If he isn't behind the notes, ghosting me is a pretty terrible thing to do, even if I did come off too heavy," she said. "All he has to do is be straightforward with me. And he seemed so honest. After a weekend with him, not responding at all is unacceptable, really."

"I agree," Marion said.

Anthony chimed in. "So do I."

Marion smiled. "That's why he has to be the one behind the notes."

Then suddenly, their first conversation floated back to Heather. "Hang on. When we met, he said there was something freeing about having no expectations with people he met on a plane." Her stomach dropped.

Marion's lips parted, and Heather could tell her attention was narrowing.

"He'd said you could be truthful, or to use his words, 'You

can be any version of yourself you want for a couple of hours... because your actions won't follow you when you land.' Then he said, 'I'll disappear into the swarms of passengers, and you'll be on your way.'"

Realization dawned. "You don't think he was pretending to be this charismatic person just to pass the time with a friendly stranger, do you?" she asked them. "And maybe he knew all along that he'd disappear and never see me again?"

"I don't know. It's hard to answer when I've never met him." Marion looked at Anthony for his view on it, and he shrugged.

Feeling exposed, Heather turned back to the view, trying to get herself together. A church sign still announced their Christmas Eve candlelight service, and a rustic nativity scene stood in the open churchyard beside a split-rail fence. Beyond the structures, the mountains loomed in a cloudy blue that blended against the sky. But that conversation went around in her head, every breath, every word under scrutiny.

While she didn't want her happiness to be wrapped up in someone else right now, her heart was fragile, and she feared that Nick's actions might have shattered her trust. He had to be behind the messages. If not, she might not recover from any other outcome. A winter wind blew through the carriage, carrying her delicate confidence with it.

Chapter Twenty-Three

The carriage came to a stop outside Mason's Bookshop. Its windows were fogged with warmth. Anthony hopped out and held out a hand to help them down. Once on the sidewalk, Marion and Heather folded their blankets and tucked them under their arms. The scent of pine drifted over from a wreath hung slightly askew on the bookshop door.

The horses shifted, their hooves clacking against the street, the bells around their necks jingling. Anthony insisted on handling payment for the driver, and then they went inside. Paper snowflakes dangled from twine above the old wooden counter, and a strand of lights glistened along varnished shelves, the edges worn smooth by decades of browsing hands. Anthony stopped in front of the business section, leaving Heather and Marion right outside a wide passageway with The Local Mug coffee shop next door, open so people could get a warm drink and settle into the oversized chairs on the Mason's side with a good book.

Outside, snow gathered along the curb, but inside, time slowed, every second lingering over paper cups of cocoa, whispered recommendations, and the gentle thrill that every gift wrapped in brown paper held a story waiting to be opened. With a loud whistle outside, the horses snapped to attention. The carriage wheels turned and soon it was out of view.

"Should we get something?" Marion asked, leaning around a few people to see the drink options through the passageway.

"A drink would warm me up for sure."

After a quick check with Anthony to see if he wanted anything, they made their way to the coffee side of the shop, where patrons gathered around steaming mugs and gooey pastries.

"I think I'm getting a cup of apple cider," Marion said. "How about you?"

Heather eyed a mug on another table—dark chocolate rimmed with whipped cream and chocolate sprinkles. "The hot cocoa looks good."

"Okay," Marion said with purpose, "I'll get our drinks. Go grab us a table if you can."

Heather accepted the mission and snaked through the small space, finding an empty table tucked away along the side shared with the bookshop. She waved to Anthony through a small open cutout, getting his attention so he'd know where they were.

A couple beside her sipped their drinks quietly, their noses in their books. She and Toby used to do that. She eyed the woman. Did she realize how lucky she was that her significant other was perfectly content to read next to her? Would Heather ever find someone she could be entirely herself with again? She'd come a long way this holiday, but Nick's silence continued to rattle her, and a sense of outrage and hurt was building.

Marion set a tray with two mugs and a plate onto the table. "I couldn't help myself." Sitting on the plate were two flaky, buttery croissants the size of her hand, filled with dark chocolate that oozed out the sides and topped with almonds, curled chocolate, and powdered sugar.

"Oh my." Heather picked one up. It was still warm. She took a bite. The chocolate had the consistency of mousse and, mixed with the crunch of the toppings and the slightly sweet and salty toasted flavor of the croissant, it was pure indulgence. She followed it with a creamy swig of rich hot cocoa. "These have to be the staple of every future girls' weekend."

"We could do some real damage in this town on a girls' weekend," Marion said, tearing a piece off her croissant and popping it into her mouth.

"We definitely could—and will!"

In all of this, Marion had been a ray of sunshine, the one constant who never failed her. She truly was the best friend a girl could have. "I'm so glad you and Anthony were able to share the holiday with me."

"Me too." Marion's gaze flitted through the open window between the shops, and she straightened, her hands stilling, her eyes widening.

"What's wrong?" Heather asked.

Marion's lips parted, but nothing came out at first, as if disbelief were stopping her. "Look at Anthony."

Heather craned her neck to see through the crowded spot in the wall's cutout until she found him, standing in front of the parenting section, leafing through a book. She sucked in her lips. "You don't think he's reading something from that shelf, do you?"

She and Marion looked back at each other in hopeful shock.

Marion squinted. "What does the book say on the front? All I can see is a blue-and-white cover."

Heather immediately recognized it and drew Marion's attention to the large sales poster. "It's that one, isn't it?"

An enormous mockup of the book was splashed on the front of the poster. The title read: *Brace Yourself: Parenting Advice from an Ex-Bachelor*.

Marion slapped her hand over her gaping mouth. "I'm not going to get my hopes up," she said through her fingers, but the look on her face said otherwise.

As the snow fell outside, they finished their nibbles and carried their mugs to the bookshop, where Anthony had moved on to the magazines. Neither of them said anything to him, and he didn't seem to know what they'd seen. Heather didn't say anything because she wouldn't want to pry, and she was willing to guess Marion didn't want to air their private business. But Heather hoped the book could provide a springboard for discussion once they were by themselves.

After they all had a book that sounded good, they grabbed a group of upholstered chairs as soon as they opened up. With another drink of her sumptuous hot cocoa, Heather opened her book and settled in to the first chapter.

"I packed a couple of books for this trip that I haven't read, but I'm going to have to get this one now," she said after finishing the chapter.

Anthony closed a self-help book on building endurance. "Marion claims that if we have some kind of local emergency where we have no power for a week, she'll need the extra book stock."

Heather laughed and set the novel in her lap. "Good point."

Marion nodded. "Thank you."

"Except she has enough"—Anthony put up air quotes—"'emergency books' to last her for the next millennium." He winked at her, and she blew him an air kiss.

"It's the downside of marrying a librarian," Heather said with a laugh.

They left their chairs and went up to the counter. Once

they'd paid for their books and returned Heather' and Marion's empty mugs to the dish bin on the other side, the three of them stepped out into the winter cold and made their way down to the art gallery at the end of the road.

Inside, the walls were cluttered with watercolors and oil paintings. Sunsets, bears roaming in the woods, a covered bridge in a snowy landscape... The paintings were labeled with a short bio of each artist. Marion took Anthony's hand as they walked through the space, reading and observing.

To give Marion and Anthony a moment, Heather went over to a painting that caught her eye—a boat in a storm. She stared at it until the colors gave way to brushstrokes, and then she focused in further and the textures emerged.

Marion joined her when Anthony went to inspect a sculpture.

"You know, if you get really close to these paintings, you just see roughness and smoothness," Heather said. "But it isn't until you pan out that you get the whole picture. Life is like that."

"That's deep." Marion stepped up to a painting and squinted at it. "I see what you mean."

What would Heather's life be like at the end, when she could pan out? Would it be a storm like this painting or would it be sunshine? Either way, she was willing to bet it would be beautiful.

They walked around until they'd finished browsing all the art in the small space.

Marion checked her watch. "We have enough time to see the chapel all decorated for Christmas before it closes. Want to go?"

"I'd love to," Heather said.

Marion beckoned Anthony. "Could you drive us to see a little church?"

"Sure. Stay here where it's warm. I'll swing around and

pick you two up." Anthony pulled his keys from his pocket and went to get his truck from down the block.

"Should I bring up the parenting book?" Marion said after he left.

Heather folded over the top of the paper bag with her book. "That's totally your call."

Marion blinked. "I mean, what was that? Is he thinking about having a baby?"

"You won't know unless you ask him."

"I'm afraid to," Marion said, her shoulders slightly raised. "Because I'd rather think he's reconsidering than to have him tell me no."

Anthony pulled up. With a hopeful bob of her eyebrows, Marion opened the door and they went back into the falling snow. Anthony drove the few streets over and parallel parked. They still had to walk a bit up the hill to the white clapboard chapel, but Heather didn't mind. With the snow, the holiday banners on light posts, and the Christmas lights, the little town had a storybook feel to it.

They walked up the hill that was littered with headstones. Marion pulled out her phone and madly typed. "I'll look up the history and be our tour guide." She stepped over a fallen branch. "Oh, this is cool." She scrolled. "This chapel is a local gathering spot for both weddings and funerals. At funerals, the chapel's bell is rung once for every year a person lived, a tradition that began in the 1800s and still continues today."

Heather ran her hand over one of the headstones, each one representing a life. This particular one was so old she could no longer read the inscription. How many bells had rung for this person? Had their life been cut short like Toby's?

If Toby had taught her one thing, it was that life could be fleeting. She didn't know how many times that bell would toll for her. So she'd better make the most of every single minute.

When they'd walked down the small aisle inside, past the

wooden pews, and had a closer look at the piano up front, Anthony picked them up and they went on the Christmas-tree walking tour. But they only saw a few lit trees before ducking out at one of the stops nearer to where Anthony had parked because they were nearly frozen.

He'd been quiet on the way home while Marion and Heather chatted away. Now, back in the cozy warmth of the cabin, he already had a game on TV and was adding a few logs to the fire while Heather set one of the platters of cookies on the coffee table. Anthony picked up Scarlett and plopped down on the sofa with her purring in his arms. Heather and Marion bent over the fireplace, warming their hands.

"My favorite place we visited today was the bookshop." Marion sat next to Anthony, draping her legs on top of his.

Heather sat down in the armchair by the sofa. "It was a perfect day." She picked up one of the cookies and nibbled its sugary edge.

Marion selected one for herself and took a bite, settling back against the sofa. Scarlett crawled off Anthony's lap and into Marion's. With a grin, she stroked the kitten.

Only then did both of them seem to notice Anthony's silence.

The game was on, but he was unusually quiet. He seemed lost in thought, not reacting to the second-yard-line drama that was playing out on the screen. His expression was somber, unlike his usual easygoing attitude.

Marion eyed Heather, but unsure why his demeanor had changed so abruptly, Heather shrugged discreetly.

Scooting closer to him, Marion rubbed his shoulder. "You okay?"

"Hm?" He cleared his throat, fiddling with the remote he'd set on the arm of the sofa. "Yeah. Why?"

"You look pensive."

When she said that, the contemplative look washed over

him again. "I don't know," he finally said. "It feels different here."

"What feels different," Marion asked as she cuddled Scarlett.

"This house feels like the kind of place a family would live in. And being here with you got me thinking about our future."

Only because Heather knew the background of this conversation did she notice the minuscule lift in Marion's body.

"What about it?" Marion asked, her words breathy.

He shook his head and faced her. "It got me wondering if all those hours at work are really what I'm supposed to be doing with my time." His gaze fell onto the coffee table, but it was as if he were looking through it. "Am I building the wrong thing?"

"What do you mean by that?"

"Maybe I should be working long hours to build something that includes you."

Her breathing became steady, her shirt slowly rising and falling. "Are you saying what I think you're saying?"

The corner of his mouth lifted. "I don't know. Maybe."

The two of them shared a quiet moment of understanding. Then Marion leaned over and kissed his cheek. "That's the best thing I think I've ever heard you say."

"This cabin is a little *too* comfortable," he said, making eye contact with Heather and pulling her into the conversation.

"I hate that we ever have to leave," Marion said. "If I were you, Heather, I'd spend every waking moment here."

Heather smiled, her heart full for her friends. "While I could stay here for the rest of the holiday, I need to get myself acclimated to regular life again before I have to go back to work." She'd like to go through Toby's things and see if she could figure out what had been sent to storage. She was ready. "I'll probably pack up tonight. I'll be leaving with a lot more than I came here with." She waggled a finger at the cookies.

"True." Marion swung her legs off Anthony. She bent down under the tree and picked up the final envelope, which had been wrapped up with the photo album. "Don't forget this."

Heather took it and held what was probably the last message from Toby in her hands. If she was truly ready to move on, she needed to enjoy it and then decide how the rest of her life would look. While there were still unanswered questions, like why Nick had been so ruthless in ignoring her, she needed to take the next step and start living again.

Slowly, savoring the moment, she picked off the green wax seal and then opened the flap, the familiar handwriting coming into focus.

"What does it say?" Marion asked.

"It says, 'I love you more than words, so I'll keep them short for this message. While you might think it's the end, it's just the beginning.'" She looked at Marion. "Even after he's gone, he can read my mind. I've been thinking about how I need to step fully into my new life." She laid her hand on his final message, which felt like his blessing.

Heather spent the rest of the evening with that thought rolling around in her head. Once everyone had gone up for the night, she lay on the comforter in her bedroom with her journal open. After a few minutes of contemplation, she wrote:

Dear Toby,
I can't express how thankful I am for all you've done for me. Only you could come back and make this happen. But I'm at a loss as to what to do

next. For a brief moment, I thought I knew, but now I'm not so sure. I suppose that, just like I did after you left us, I'll put one foot in front of another and blindly take the next step until it becomes clear.

Love you.

She closed the book and set it on the nightstand. The unknown was uncomfortable, but it was all she had now, so she'd better get used to the feeling.

Chapter Twenty-Four

The next day, after a big breakfast, Heather and Marion sorted the food, placing cold items in Anthony's cooler to get them home and packing the rest in bags and loading them into Heather's car. Anthony had let the fire in the fireplace burn down and was using the poker to flatten the embers.

When they'd packed, turned off all the lights, and locked up, they said their goodbyes.

"I'll run all the cold food over to you once we get home," Marion said, holding Scarlett's carrier.

"Thanks." Heather put her hands on her hips and surveyed the cabin. *Well, Toby, this is it.*

Marion took a step toward Heather and put her arm around her. "See you when we get home."

"Okay, drive carefully." Heather stroked the kitten's head through the grate.

"You too. Follow us home if you want to. We'll make sure to wait for you as we go."

"That would be great in this weather."

They got in their vehicles and began the long drive back to

Nashville. The whole way, Heather's mind was swimming with all she'd done over the holiday. What had started as a dreaded few weeks of grief had turned into something so much better, thanks to Toby.

The only question left was Nick. But she was starting to believe it wasn't really a question at all. He'd made things pretty clear with his silence. She hated that what they'd started would end with her never knowing. Even if he wasn't truthful, she wanted to know, and she was angry with him for putting her through this, knowing what she'd dealt with.

She was also upset with herself for believing so easily that he'd been a good guy. Apparently, she had a lot to learn before getting back into the dating world. The only silver lining was that she hadn't had time to cry over her complete lack of judgment. Toby had kept her too busy. But she did worry about what might happen emotionally once she was back in her quiet apartment.

When she pulled into her parking deck, it was nearly dinnertime. She unloaded her car and went inside. Without unpacking, looking for dinner options, she dug into the bags of dry food Anthony had packed into her car for her, but all she had were cookies, crackers, and chips since Anthony had taken the cold items home.

She started loading the snacks into her pantry and was thinking of calling in some Chinese food when her phone rang. She didn't know the number. Hoping it might be Nick on a new phone or something, she answered.

"This is Alex Branson from *People's Entertainment*. I'm calling back to see if this is a better time."

She should've marked his number when he'd made the last call. Weren't the days between Christmas and New Year's still the holiday? Did these people ever take time off work?

"I know you said you'd like to keep your life private, and we are aware of the fact that Toby did as well, but there's been a development that I think you might want to weigh in on, and I was hoping to get a quote from you as to how you feel about it."

She stopped unpacking, a bag of pretzels in her hand. "What development?"

"My circles are abuzz about a project that's supposed to be a new perspective on Toby's life, and we were hoping to give you the opportunity to set the record straight and provide your side of the story. We aren't sure exactly what information will be released, but we wanted to verify a few details regarding Toby's cancer and what the battle was like from your perspective."

She barely heard what he was saying, her mind snagging on his mention of "a new perspective." How would anyone have any real perspective at all on Toby's life? Certainly, any secondhand information would be full of holes and only partial truths.

"Someone's doing a story on Toby without having requested an interview with *me*?"

"That's right."

She hadn't considered that if she didn't answer all those calls, people might try to take matters into their own hands. She'd need to try to stop them. "What kind of piece is it—an article, television news spot? Do you know anything about it?"

"We have reason to believe that an anonymous donor paid fifty thousand dollars to commission a biography of Toby Hart's rise to fame and his life behind the spotlight, including his battle with cancer, and the book is releasing soon."

Her pulse rose in her ears. "Fifty thousand dollars?" That was a lot of money. The donor had to be a pretty big organization, right? "Where did you get this information?"

"I can't reveal a whole lot on that. A source that shall remain nameless overheard a phone call between the donor and the author of the biography, and we've been digging ever since. The publisher is tight-lipped and won't give us any information, and the author isn't returning our calls, so it would be incredibly helpful to hear the truth from you."

She set the bag of pretzels on the counter, her hunger pains long gone. Instead, she felt sick. Toby would never have wanted a biography chronicling his illness to be on the market, and he surely wouldn't want his personal life on display.

"Who's the publisher?"

"Iron Pen Creative."

"I've never heard of them."

"They're small. Independent. And the author is relatively unknown. He's never written in this genre that we can find."

This news slowly began to take hold in her mind. So some large entity was commissioning this biography and using a small publisher and a nobody author? Why? Because they were spreading lies that no larger publisher or seasoned biographer would write? How ruthless.

"Can you disclose the name of the author?" Perhaps they'd tried to call her for an interview and she'd recognize the name. At the very least, if she had a name, she could find them and try to stop them from publishing the book.

"His name is Nicholas Monroe."

Her heart stopped. She didn't hear a word of what came next, her every moment with Nick flashing before her eyes.

He'd said he worked in research. *"I've dabbled in fiction and a few nonfiction projects, but I haven't published anything... Lately, I haven't been able to do as much writing as I want to. Maybe I will when I get home."*

Toby's life was the project he'd been working on? Had Nick been following her and somehow found out she'd be on that plane to Greenville? Was that why he'd been a perfect gentleman, because he'd been creating scenarios so he could talk to her?

She immediately went into panic mode, trying to recall every detail of the conversations she'd had with him, seeing them all in a new light. His voice had sounded familiar, and now she was getting a squirming feeling that he'd spoken to her on the phone before they'd met. And that same voice had called another time.

"Hi. Don't hang up. I'm writing about Toby—"

Definitely not. She cut him off. "Toby made it clear that he didn't want the attention to be on anything but his music."

This whole time, he'd been writing about Toby?

Surely this wasn't true...

But slowly, the events that had her walking on cloud nine now had her free falling. He hadn't asked her last name at the pizza restaurant in Greenville. She'd thought he was being considerate. But it was because he already knew it. Those moments when it looked like he wanted to tell her something —had the words on his lips been guilty confessions? And that meeting he'd had—was that to discuss what he'd found out with the donor?

Now she understood why he hadn't called her. Because he'd clearly gotten whatever it was he'd needed from her. She felt sick.

"Hello?" Alex Branson's voice slid down the line and back into her consciousness.

"Sorry," she said, breathless, tears clouding her vision. She swallowed, trying but failing to muster all her strength. "Do you know where I can find this Nicholas Monroe?" Her voice shook.

"I do, actually. We looked him up."

"You have his address?" She swallowed against her dry mouth and wiped a runaway tear from her cheek.

"Yep."

She scrambled around the other side of the kitchen bar and frantically dug through her junk drawer for a pad of paper and a pen. When she'd managed to find both through the blindness of her tears, she scratched down the address and read it back to him.

"Could we get a statement from you at least?" Alex asked.

"Yeah. The people involved in this are crooks."

With a trembling hand, she ended the call and set the phone on the counter in a haze of confusion. She paced the kitchen, squeezing her eyes shut and willing the dizziness from her head. She bent over and put her hands on her knees, her back heaving as her heart shattered. Nick had broken her trust in the biggest way—he'd lied to her face. And she'd believed it.

Her body locked in the pain of his deception and betrayal. Indignation boiled over like a forgotten pot on the stove. She'd quietly sat there, day after day, worrying she'd said something wrong. She'd made excuses for him, chalking his silence up to the holidays, and all along he'd only been pretending to have an interest in her. And he'd had the audacity to prey on a grieving widow's loneliness. That phone number he'd given her probably wasn't even his. How could she ever trust anyone after this?

Looking back with this new information, it was ridiculous for her to think that Mr. Perfect would magically show up on a flight, woo her, and they'd live happily ever after. He'd taken fifty thousand dollars to write a book about her that he had surely known she wouldn't approve of after cutting him off on the phone whenever he'd called. He hadn't gotten a clue from her telling him she wasn't interested, and she'd hung up on him at least once. And yet, he was still going through with writing it. Even worse, he'd known that and still flashed that adorable grin at her, flirted with her, and used his dog to melt her heart.

Leaving all her bags where they were, she went into her bedroom and fell onto her bed. She buried her head in the pillow and sobbed. She'd barely recovered after Toby's death and in that one phone call, what she'd learned about Nick had crushed any progress she'd made. How could she trust her own judgment after this? She'd thought he was a decent person. She'd opened up to him in a way she'd never done with anyone before, and he'd trampled all over her trust.

But also, there was the pain of falling for someone who didn't return her feelings. There was no one to protect her heart.

Alone and broken, she cried herself to sleep.

Chapter Twenty-Five

When the sun peeked through the clouds the next day, Heather rolled over and groaned. She felt as if she'd been hit by a truck. Her whole body ached from stress, and her head pounded. She hadn't experienced this since the weeks right after Toby's death, and she recognized the sensation easily—it was the response to loss. But in this case, with Nick, how could she lose something she never really had?

She closed her stinging, puffy eyes and punched her pillow into shape, hoping the new, elevated position would ease the ache in her neck, but it didn't. She was broken once again. But this was different from the last time because her ability to believe people was what was broken now. Doing this to someone who was already vulnerable, and at Christmas, was heartless. She couldn't believe it. And here she'd been, making excuses for Nick's silence, giving him the benefit of the doubt, and hoping he was the one sending love letters from Toby, while in reality, he couldn't care less about her.

Her lip wobbled, and the ache in her chest built. Nick had wrecked her. And for what—a book? He was a nobody right now, but this book would certainly propel him to fame. His career was more important than a human heart. He was the absolute opposite of Toby. And she'd fallen for it.

After tossing and turning in bed, trying and failing to find sleep, she got up and wandered into the living room. Her things were still strewn about, the place a mess. She stepped over her suitcases and went into the kitchen. Her bags of groceries from the cabin were sitting on the floor. She stood in the middle of the room, unsure why she'd even come in. Her body was reacting to the habit of making coffee first thing, but she didn't want any.

She needed to talk to her best friend—the one person she could trust. The other option was her mom, but it would take too long to explain it all to her, and she didn't know if she could make it through the entire story. Also, Marion would know what to say. She got her phone off the kitchen counter and called her friend.

When Marion answered, Heather burst into tears, unable to control her emotions, and told her what she'd found out.

"What?" Marion's voice screeched through the phone. "Oh my gosh, Heather. I'm so sorry."

"I don't know how to move forward," she blubbered, empty. "Do I try to go to the publisher first? Do I go to Nick's? I won't be able to talk without breaking down."

"Is this even legal? Let me go get Anthony. I'll put you on speaker."

Heather grabbed a tissue from the box on the counter and wiped her tears as Marion regurgitated the situation to Anthony. "Could it be an invasion of privacy?" Heather asked.

"Well, yes and no. He can write an unauthorized biography. The First Amendment offers broad protection for writing factually about a public figure."

More tears spilled over Heather's lashes, blurring her vision. She pulled another tissue from the box.

"You *could* sue for defamation," Anthony continued, "but only if false or damaging statements are published. Keep in mind, though, that a public figure would have to prove actual malice, and usually defamation and privacy claims don't survive death, so with Toby not here to claim it, you might be out of luck."

She balled up the tissue and wiped her nose. "Is there any way to bring him to justice for this? It seems so wrong, given how he coerced me into telling him things."

"You could claim invasion of privacy if the author discloses private facts that aren't legitimate public interest or if he obtained his information through illegal means."

"Like lying?" she asked.

"Writing a biography based on facts obtained through deception isn't considered an invasion of privacy in a legal sense. I think the legal issue would be the disclosure of private facts, but not the method of gathering the information."

Heather sighed. "And we won't know if he's disclosed anything private until the book is out there."

"I'll keep thinking," Anthony said. "Sorry you're dealing with this. And if we can come up with a way to sue him, I'll represent you free of charge."

"That's really thoughtful—thank you." She was so glad to have Marion and Anthony on her side.

Marion turned the phone off speaker and came back on the line. "I feel terrible."

"It isn't your fault."

"But I told you Nick was exactly the kind of guy you should be talking to."

"How were you to know? I was the one talking to him, and *I* couldn't even see it." She tossed the tissues into the trash can. "The thing is, I could deal with there being a book about Toby. I don't love the idea, and I know Toby would hate it, but it's about being lied to. I was so excited to feel something other than grief that I think I'd have believed anything." Her throat began to close as a lump formed. "I actually wrote to Toby in my journal that just when I was starting to move forward, his notes would pull me back to my old life, and I'd miss him all over again. There were moments when I actually wanted the notes to stop for *Nick*. I was willing to push Toby's memory away for someone I met over a weekend. What kind of person does that?"

"You're being way too hard on yourself," Marion said.

"Am I?"

"Yes. You wanted the notes to stop because you were giving yourself the chance to move forward, and that's a difficult task given how devoted you were to Toby. It actually shows an incredible feat by you to take a leap when you weren't sure what was next—and moving without planning is something you always struggle with."

"Thank you for talking me through it," she said with a sniffle.

"Of course. Do you want me to come over?"

Heather looked around at the mess. "I don't know. I still need to unpack... But thank you for offering."

"Are you going to confront Nick?"

"I might have to if I want to try to keep this book from coming out."

"If you need me for support, you call me right away," Marion said. "Do you think it's safe to confront him? If he'd lie to your face, would he be capable of anything else?"

"I can't imagine he'd hurt me in any way." But if she were being honest, she didn't know. She didn't know Nick at all, apparently.

"I'll keep my phone on me," Marion said. "Call immediately if you need me."

"Okay."

They said their goodbyes and Heather found herself alone

once more. With a deep breath, she began picking up the house, her every movement as if on autopilot. She started with the food from the cabin, unloading bags and putting things away in her pantry. When she got that done, she unzipped her suitcase and made piles of dirty laundry.

As she loaded the washing machine, she couldn't help but consider the two extremes of her holiday. Thank goodness for Toby's notes. Had she dealt with the disclosure of this book without having Toby's quiet support and outpouring of love, she might not have made it. Although she was still broken-hearted, Toby had saved her because she knew that, while the rest of the world seemed cruel, he'd been with her even in death. He'd always be with her—the notes were her one truth this Christmas.

Chapter Twenty-Six

By midday, Heather had finally stopped crying. The house was clean, and she'd finished the last load of laundry. She'd managed to keep down a couple crackers, but her stomach was unsettled after everything she'd dealt with.

Nick's address sat on the coffee table. She stared at it, hollow and empty. How could he have been so cold? He'd made her feel comfortable and, by the flight home, she'd fallen right into his hands. Had he stalked her prior to the flight, following her around town? Did he know where she lived? The idea gave her a shiver.

Well, two could play at that game. She stood up and got her keys and phone. Then, with an angry swipe, she grabbed his address off the table. Time to snoop and see what Nick Monroe was up to. And maybe, if she could muster enough courage, she'd confront him.

She left her apartment and headed for Nick's. With the address in her navigation, directions chirping away, she called Marion.

"I'm en route to Nick's," she said.

“Sure you want to go by yourself?”

“I’ll be fine. I’m irate enough to take him down.”

“I can see the headline: ‘Local Librarian Goes Rogue.’”

Even in this awful situation, Marion could get her to smile —if only briefly.

“I need to see him now I have a full understanding of his motives. He can’t hurt me anymore.”

“What are you going to do when you get there?” Marion asked.

“I don’t know. Right now, I want to see where he lives, if there’s any evidence of him having a dog and living the way he told me he did. Although, I don’t know why I care. If he lied about what he was writing, it doesn’t matter if the rest is a lie.”

“Why check then?”

“I guess some part of me wants him to be a good guy, even though I know he isn’t. At the very least, I’d like to see him cuddling his dog—so I know he isn’t totally heartless. It’s ridiculous, I know.”

“That’s the optimist in you. You want people to be inherently good.”

Heather made a turn and drove down a side street lined with bungalows. “I’m usually a decent judge of character. He didn’t seem like an awful person.”

“You told him who you were. He knew full well what he wasn’t telling you.”

“I know. It’s so baffling.”

“You can’t fathom it because you’re a good person,” Marion said. “But not everyone has your standards.”

“Clearly. The entity paying for the biography, Nick, and probably the publisher are all shady people if they’re doing this without my knowledge. Not one of them, that I’m aware of, has contacted me except Nick. And when I told him I wasn’t interested and didn’t take his calls, he resorted to devious tactics to get what he wanted. Why can't people just leave me alone?"

"I don't know why people do what they do."

"Wait," Heather whispered, slowing down. She pulled over in front of a bungalow down the street from Nick's and turned off her car to be inconspicuous. Her heart pattered in her chest. "I see him."

"What's he doing?"

"He's getting the mail." She squinted down the street, and her heart skipped a beat, seeing him again. Her buried emotions hadn't caught up with the fact that he was a total jerk.

He went around the side of the house.

"He's out of view. Let me move closer." She started the engine and shifted into drive.

"Be careful."

Slowly, she drove toward his residence, unable to see him. She moved nearer to the driveway, then slouched down and decelerated to a roll.

"See anything?"

"A shadow crossed through the front window, and I think I saw a dog jump up." That was promising. At least he was truthful about Ophelia.

But when she got to the other side of the driveway, with a gasp, she slammed on her brakes, the car jerking to a stop in the middle of the road.

"What? Tell me."

It felt as if the blood was draining from her body. *What does this mean?*

"What is it, Heather?" Marion's voice pushed through.

"Um..." She struggled to get her mind around what she'd seen. Her mouth was dry, her heart hammering, her fingers trembling. "He has a..." She couldn't breathe, she was lightheaded.

"A what?"

"He drives a white Suburban." Her emotions became a tidal wave that overpowered her, sending her to the darkest depths of the ocean. In that moment, she wanted to rewind time and take back her wish that Nick had been behind the notes.

"Go to The Steaming Quill right now. I'll meet you there."

Forcing herself to see the road through her tears, she punched the gas and didn't look back. As she drove, a question ballooned in her mind. She tried not to let it push through, but it was relentless. What if the notes, too, had all been a lie? Had Nick somehow gotten Toby's personal things —maybe he came by when Toby's nurse was with him, claiming to be a friend or something. Why would he do that? Unless that was how he'd gotten what he needed for the book. Anxiety from such a deception pulsed through her.

In a few minutes, she was locating parallel parking options outside the coffee shop. She squeezed into a nonexistent spot and got out. Marion was already walking toward her and ushering her into the building. Heather went inside, dazed.

"Go sit. I'll get us each a coffee," Marion said.

Her mind going a hundred miles an hour, Heather found a seat at a table in the corner of the shop, away from other patrons.

A white SUV had been at the tree lot. It had sped off so they wouldn't see who was in it. And then, on the way to the cabin, she'd seen a white SUV again. If he had those personal details, what else did he have? *How* did he get that information from Toby? Even in his darkest hours, Toby would never have divulged anything. She racked her brain.

Suddenly, more became clear. Stargate Publishing had a last-minute request from someone who'd written something about Toby and needed to double-check their copyright information for a couple of his songs before it was distributed. Books had copyrights. Would Stargate Publishing have sold that person his songs for a price, and that was how she'd received the uncut sheet music?

How had Nick found out that she loved the meatloaf casserole? That Toby had done all the cooking? She'd delivered that casserole to so many people. All it took was Nick asking around and one person revealing that, and he had enough to create a recipe book. While they were delicious, the sugar cookies hadn't been the same as Toby's. She'd chalked the difference up to her lack of baking practice, but now she wondered if the recipe had been his at all.

And what about the photos in the album? A fuzzy memory returned.

"What's that box outside the door?" she asked Toby, coming home from work one day. It was sealed shut and had the words "For Pick Up" written in Toby's scratchy and nearly illegible handwriting.

"Oh, more files I'm putting into storage. I've got a guy picking them up."

Then, he'd gotten really sick, and she'd never followed up to see who the courier was. Did the correct person take it? Or had someone else swiped it—someone like Nick? Toby said himself that they didn't have enough security in that building. Would the photos from her album or the cabin key and unpublished songs have inadvertently been put into the box? How long had Nick been planning this to get what he needed?

She wondered again if he'd been watching her. He could've been in the cabin. Were there cameras in there to record her reaction? Her mind went wild with what-ifs.

When Marion returned with their coffees, she unloaded everything she'd pieced together.

Marion stared at her, eyes wide. "Well, if you wanted a reason to sue him, I'd think you'd have one. That is, if you could prove any of it." She scooted her drink out of the way and leaned forward. "Do you think he's really capable of all that?"

"A week ago, I'd have said absolutely not, but I don't know what to believe anymore."

She held in her tears, but they'd be coming soon enough.

Chapter Twenty-Seven

Heather hadn't let it all really sink in until she got home, but once she'd left Marion and was back in the quiet of her apartment, she fell to the floor, sobbing. She'd been there for the last few hours. Marion had offered to come back with her, but she'd said she wanted to be alone.

What she'd refused to think about at any length until this moment was the actual fact that Toby hadn't really planned anything for her this year. The notes were never from him. She closed her eyes, the silence that had been there since his last breath suffocating her now. She wanted answers as to why Nick would do this to her, but with every new detail she got, she was more devastated. He had managed to make an already heart-wrenching holiday unbearable. He'd ripped her heart in two, and she didn't know how to pick up the pieces. But it wasn't over. That book would come out, slashing open the wounds of this deception every time she saw it in the stores.

If she were being honest with herself, Nick creating the messages made the most sense. How could Toby have planned all that, given how sick he was? Her one last truth of Toby's final act of love had been shattered. Nick had completely broken her. And for what? Money?

Her journal responses to Toby about his messages were useless now. She hadn't been talking to Toby. She'd been replying to Nick, a dishonest, devious person.

Nick had toyed with her emotions, preying on her sadness. Given the depth of his scheme, what other lies was he planning to publish in that book? Would she have more battles to face? Would she end up fighting for Toby's reputation? Just the idea of it exhausted her.

She had to get herself together and confront him.

Eventually, the tears subsided the angrier she got. There was no way she was going to let him think he could get away with this. She was going to demand that he abandon the book, or she'd take him to court.

She wiped her eyes with her forearm, a new sense of determination driving her. She ran her fingers through her hair, went into the bathroom, and got herself together. She straightened her sweater and jeans and looked at herself in the mirror—decent enough. Then she left her apartment, got back in the car, and drove over to Nick's.

She seethed for the entire fifteen-minute drive, going over scenarios of what she'd say once she was face-to-face with him. He'd hurt her in unimaginable ways and she was absolutely crushed, but she had to have enough courage to give him a piece of her mind, and she'd let her anger achieve that.

Once she arrived at his house, she pulled into the driveway and got out of the car. With a rigidity to her steps, she made her way to the front door and rang the bell.

Ophelia barked inside.

The door opened, and Nick's face lit up when he saw her, his wide smile emerging—still playing the part. "Hey," he said, wonderment in his eyes as he searched her face.

"Don't give me that," she spat as she pushed past him into the house.

Ophelia barked at her.

She reached out a hand to the dog and the dog growled.

"Even the stories of your sweet dog were fake."

"What?" Nick pawed at the dog, looking confused.

Ophelia barked at her incessantly, despite his attempts to calm her down.

"Ophelia," he commanded. "Settle." But she wouldn't stop barking.

"Adorable," Heather snapped.

"She's protective, and you're coming in like an erupting volcano. What in the world is going on?"

He tried to take her coat, but she refused, lurching away from his grip.

"Where should I begin?" she said. "We'll start basic. You ghosted me after we got home."

"I assumed *you* ghosted *me*. You never texted me," he said, hooking a finger into Ophelia's collar, the dog relentless.

Another lie.

"Yes, I certainly did," Heather said, pulling up her unanswered texts and showing him.

His brows pulled together. He went over to the sofa and patted for Ophelia to join him. She obeyed, her suspicious gaze lingering on Heather. He gestured toward another chair, but Heather remained standing. With him sitting, Ophelia's barking finally subsided.

"I never got them," he said.

The honesty in his eyes made her falter. She peered at her two messages. Each one had appeared to send, settling quietly into the empty thread. There was no warning, no error, just her two texts suspended on her phone alone, unseen and unread on the other side.

"How could you not have gotten them? And even if you didn't, I know you had my number. Why didn't you call me?"

"You know I had your number?" he asked, his smile fading.

Got him.

"You called me twice about Toby, and I told you I wasn't interested."

"How did you know that was me?" he inquired, asking her again to sit.

She ignored his suggestion.

"I did try to call. Only once." His voice was softer. "At first, I thought you were busy with the holiday, but days went by and I missed you. I called, but it went straight to voicemail. I didn't leave a message. After all you'd told me about losing your husband, I figured you'd changed your mind and didn't want to talk to me, so I was giving you time."

"I didn't get a notification that you called at all."

His face crumpled. "That's so weird. Could I see your phone?"

She pulled back. "No."

"It's like you blocked me or something."

Understanding dawned.

"Hi. Don't hang up. I'm writing about Toby—"

She'd told him she wasn't interested, hung up the phone, and blocked his number.

"I think I did block you, actually," she said. "When you called saying you were writing something about Toby."

He blew air through his lips. "Well, I'm glad we got that worked out."

"Okay, so what? I blocked you. That doesn't add up to even an inkling of what you've put me through."

He stared at her, his lips parted, looking completely baffled. Playing the innocent woe-is-me card. *Unbelievable.*

"A reporter called me yesterday. He said he got a tip.

Someone overheard you and another person on the phone. I know an anonymous donor paid fifty thousand dollars to commission a biography about Toby that *you* are writing. Want to tell me why you failed to mention this on the plane?"

Clearly caught, he closed his eyes and hung his head. Then, with labored movements, he addressed her. "Heather. Please. Sit down."

With daggers in her gaze, reluctantly, and still bundled up in her coat and scarf, she sat, but only because her knees were knocking from confronting him.

Ophelia jumped off the sofa and came over, sniffing her hand. The dog looked up at her with big brown eyes. It wasn't the dog's fault her owner was a con man. Heather reached down and stroked her head.

"I was trying to avoid this very issue," he said.

"You *lied* to me?"

"I didn't lie. I was only supposed to make sure you were okay. I was late getting on the plane because I was organizing things for once we arrived in Greenville. I debated on whether to talk to you or not, but you seemed so flustered when you dropped your book that I wanted to put you at ease. After many hours spent kicking myself, I realized I probably should have stayed quiet and not talked at all, but I was overcompensating because I don't play things off well." He got up and kneeled in front of her. "But you were so adorably a mess. I just wanted to see you smile... Everything I ever said to you was the absolute truth."

Emotion welled up, despite her attempt to push it down. She wasn't going to let him continue to lie to her. She was onto him now. "So all the notes were your handiwork?"

His gaze shifted to the floor. "I coordinated everything, yes."

"The notes weren't Toby's handwriting?"

He shook his head. "I wrote the notes."

She sucked in a sob. "Why did you do that? Why did you make a grieving widow believe she was getting gifts from her deceased husband? That's the cruelest thing anyone could ever do." Tears streamed down her cheeks. "And all for *money*? Was the book so important that you could wreck someone over it? How could you?"

Nick attempted to wipe her tears, but she batted him away and stood up, folding her arms.

Ophelia barked again.

Nick righted himself and faced her. "I was *asked* to send you the notes. And there's no money involved. The reporter was wrong. The donor *offered*, but he didn't pay out."

She looked up. "Why?"

"Because I wouldn't take it. I only took the money I needed to get the job done."

Did he really think that having some sort of moment of moral thought, feeling bad, and not taking the full payment would somehow make this all okay? She didn't understand, but she didn't care to know the details of payment anyway.

"Who's the anonymous donor? Tell me."

He locked eyes with her and gritted his teeth. "I can't tell you." He ran his fingers through his hair. "Things weren't meant to happen this way, and I want to get this right. I'm trying to do what's best for everyone."

"Everyone?" she snapped. "The only one who matters in this situation is *me*. It's *my* husband's story!" She wanted to grab his shirt in her fists. "At the very least, you can't publish this with no real facts."

"I have all the facts I need. Heather, please don't get upset. I promise, everything will be okay."

She let go of him. "No. It won't."

He paced the room, went over to the window, and looked out at the view. Ophelia followed him, sitting next to his feet.

"What if I told you that I think Toby would be okay with this?"

"I'd tell you you're wrong. You don't know Toby, and you don't have a clue what he'd want."

"After writing this book, I know a lot more than you think."

Her forehead ached with grief. He didn't know anything. "You're a liar if you think you know enough about Toby's life to write an entire book. At the end of it all, that part seems to stick. You're a liar," she said again.

He came over to her. "I'm not lying."

He might have been able to deceive her before, but when it came to who knew Toby better, she had that one in the bag. There was no way Nick could convince her that Toby wanted this. Toby had told her himself that *she'd* be the one to decide when and if his story was told. And Toby would never have been okay with a fifty-thousand-dollar offer that didn't go straight to Heather. And the last thing she wanted to do was spend the foreseeable future doing damage control for Toby's legacy because of some book full of fabrications.

"What can I do to stop this project?" she asked.

"You don't need to stop it. You can't anyway."

"I'll sue if I have to."

He leaned in. "Don't go spending your time and money on a lawyer. This will all be over on New Year's Eve."

"What?" She had to force herself to breathe. "What do you mean it'll all be over?"

He gently took her shoulders, those green eyes pleading. "The book will be in print on New Year's Eve."

"How? Aren't you writing it?"

"I finished writing it six months ago—we rushed it. The edits are in and everything. And once you see it—"

"I don't want any part of it!" She worked to keep herself from breaking down right there in his living room. "If you supposedly care for me, tell me everything right now. And help me stop this."

"I promise I'll tell you everything on December 31st."

She clenched her jaw, trying not to scream at him. His loyalty was to this book over her, and the fake worry in his green eyes couldn't change that.

"I'm leaving, and if I see you again, it'll be in court."

"Heather—"

He reached for her arm, but she jerked it away. She ran outside and over to her car while he chased her. She shut the door in his face and started the engine.

"Heather, I adore you!" he called from the other side of the car's window.

She cut her eyes at him and put the car in reverse. He wasn't going to use that charm on her anymore. How self-absorbed was he to think that a counterfeit profession of love could change how she felt right now? He'd not shied away from lying before, so why would she believe him anyway?

He stared at her through the window, and he was so convincing she had to look away. As she backed out, he called, "At least unblock me!"

Little chance of that.

Chapter Twenty-Eight

Overwhelmed when she got home, Heather had gone straight to her room and lain in bed, her mind overloaded, and eventually fell asleep. The next morning, she still hadn't moved, her busy thoughts picking right back up where they'd left off the minute she'd fallen unconscious.

She reached over and checked her phone. Two missed calls from Marion. She texted that she was up and would call her soon, and then pushed the phone away from her on the nightstand.

Then she went right back to ruminating. Nick had said he could tell her everything on December 31st. That meant she probably had today and tomorrow to figure out how to stop the publication of a book. Surely they were already printed and shipped to stores, probably sitting in the back rooms, waiting to be stocked on shelves for the New Year. How could she get them pulled?

Dragging her heavy body out of bed, she got up, grabbed her phone, and went into the living room. At the back of the room, on her little desk, sat her laptop and the journal Marion had gotten her. The journal sat there as if mocking her, whispering, *How could you have been so stupid to believe the lies?* She swallowed the lump in her throat.

With a few taps on her computer, she searched: *How can you stop the publication of a book?* But the answer she got didn't offer a lot of help. Basically, like Anthony had said, she had to prove defamation. That or copyright infringement. Neither of which she could verify. With a loud exhale, she continued to scroll, searching for any loophole she could find, but there didn't seem to be one. She had nothing to take Nick to court for. She couldn't sue him for being a terrible person.

She laid her hand on the journal and looked up at the ceiling. "Oh, Toby, I'm so sorry," she said out loud, hopelessness lingering in her chest.

With a sigh, she called Marion and filled her in on her altercation with Nick, and how she realized she'd blocked his number, but now she was glad she had.

"Toby would hate to have a book about his life for everyone to weigh in on, not to mention there's the issue of whether the facts are even remotely correct," she told Marion.

"I know. You two never shared anything. So how does he even know what to write?"

"I don't have a clue." With the phone on speaker, she went into the kitchen and mindlessly poured water into the coffeemaker, more so to have some semblance of normalcy. But she didn't even really want a cup. "What's killing me the most is that Toby didn't send those notes. Nick admitted to doing it." Her voice broke and she bit her lip to keep it from wobbling.

"What a terrible thing to do to someone," Marion said.

Heather got a mug from the cabinet. "And the scary thing is those notes were so personal that I thought they were actually from Toby. How did Nick know those things?"

"No idea. What was his purpose in writing them?" Marion asked.

"I've been asking myself the same thing. Why did he bother to even talk to me on the plane if the book was finished? At least whatever I said to him won't be printed. But it doesn't make any sense." She loaded the grounds into the basket of the coffeemaker. "And I have this sinking anxiety that I've let Toby down."

"You didn't do this," Marion said. "You had no part in it."

"The release of this book feels like a freight train that I can't stop. Toby always said there wasn't enough security in our building. Will people want to verify the details in this book? Will they know where I live and try to come find me for comment? My mind is going crazy with the possibilities."

"You could always ask at the bookstore. Maybe they'd let you get an early copy, and you could start a defamation case before it comes out."

"Even if I found something, would they be able to pull them off every shelf nationwide in two days? I don't think so."

The coffeemaker beeped. Still considering ideas, she poured a cup of coffee and added milk and sugar.

Then her doorbell rang.

"Hey, there's someone at the door. Let me get that. I'll call you back."

"Okay. Be careful!"

"I will."

Through the peephole, a delivery person stood on the other side. When she opened the door, he held out a large bouquet of red roses, accented with fresh evergreen stems of pine and fir, along with red berries and sprigs of baby's breath. "Heather Hart?"

"Yes."

"These are for you."

She took the bouquet. "Thank you."

Balancing the large arrangement in one arm, she shut the door and took in the bouquet's clean, wintery scent as she carried it to the table. She plucked the card from the holder and read:

I MISS YOU ALREADY. UNBLOCK ME. I'LL EXPLAIN.

NICK

So he did know where she lived. Of course he did. He'd been the one who'd mailed her first letter from Toby. Abandoning her coffee and the roses, she went over to her desk and took the envelopes out of her journal. Gently, she took out the notes and reread the messages.

Some of the notes had little bits she was certain would be quite difficult for anyone else to know. She opened her browser and typed the question: *How do authors of unauthorized biographies gather information?* The answer that came up was typical—*public records and third-party interviews*—but the last line struck her: *They avoid making false claims, invading privacy through the use of private facts, or implying endorsement of any kind.*

Private facts? What were all these notes? They certainly were private.

She dialed Marion.

"Can you ask Anthony a legal question for me?"

"Sure, what's up?"

"Nick admitted to writing the notes from Toby, right?" Heather said, thinking aloud.

"Yeah."

"If those notes have private facts about Toby and me, and he could've known them for some time and used them in the book, could we get him on having those private facts?"

"Let me ask." Marion's distant voice came through the phone as she called Anthony over and filled him in. She put him on speaker.

"Hey," Anthony said. "So you're asking if it's legal to have obtained private information that's not in the public domain, right?"

"Yes." She hung on his silence.

"Possibly," he said. "If the letters aren't public knowledge and were obtained without your consent, then he might have violated privacy laws. But without him offering that information to anyone but you, and with no blackmail or coercion, unless it's actually written in the book, I don't think you'd have much of a case. You could file a police report and maybe request a restraining order if you're worried about stalking or harassment."

She peered at the beautiful bouquet of roses. "He hasn't really done anything that would be clearly stalking or harassment."

"Your case is pretty thin, I'd think, but you can always threaten it. Maybe he'll give you more information about the book if you send him a legal letter. I can whip one up on my letterhead."

"Thanks, Anthony. I'll hold off for now, but that's good to know."

"No problem. I'll give you back to Marion now."

The phone went off speaker and Marion returned.

"The knock at the door was a florist delivery. He just sent me an incredible bouquet of roses and said he'd explain. Maybe he's ready to talk."

"Call him," Marion said. "It's worth a shot."

"I think I'm going to find the number for Stargate Publishing, too. If they're not all home for the holidays, I'll see if they can give me any new information about the person who called them for the copyright information.

Maybe someone there has insight into what might be in the book."

"Let me know if you need me."

"Okay, thanks. I'll keep you posted."

She ended the call and immediately dialed Alice Beckmeyer at Stargate Publishing. To her disbelief, she got through to her. They said their hellos.

"It's been a long time. How are you, Heather?" Alice asked.

"I'm good," she lied for brevity. "I'm surprised to find you in the office between Christmas and New Year's."

"It's the quietest time to work. I actually get ahead," Alice said. "What's up?"

"You called a while back because you had a request for release of information from someone who was writing something about Toby."

"Oh yes. I remember," Alice said.

"Do you have the name of the person who called?"

"Let me look. Hang on just a second."

After a few minutes, she came back.

"It was a Mr. Nicholas Monroe. He wanted to double-check permission for a line of lyrics."

Hearing Nick's name on Alice's tongue made Heather's skin crawl. Her shoulders fell. "Okay, thank you."

"Did you want me to give him access to any records?"

"No, I think he has what he needs now."

"Let me know if there's anything else we can do. And congratulations on Toby's number one this season. We're all really excited."

"Thank you." She got off the phone and tapped her fingers on the desk. She'd been hoping to get the name of the donor, but he or she clearly wanted to be completely unknown. The only person who had any answers, apparently, was Nick. She considered calling him to ask more about the lyrics and why he needed them, but after everything that had transpired, she couldn't believe a word he said anyway.

Unsure what to do now, she left her desk and went back to bed.

❄

That evening, there was another knock on the door. With a twinge of anxiety, Heather pulled herself out of bed and checked the peephole.

Marion.

With relief, she opened the door.

"Yep. That's exactly what I thought." Marion brushed past her into the apartment, carrying the cooler full of refrigerator items from the cabin.

Heather closed the door and followed her to the kitchen. "What did you think?"

"That you'd be wallowing." She stopped unzipping the cooler and held up a finger. "I'm not saying that you shouldn't be wallowing, but I knew you would be." She pulled out the items and stuck them in the fridge as if she lived there. Then she went into the living room and plopped down on the sofa.

Heather lowered herself beside her. "I think I was better off crying over my wedding video at the beginning of break."

"Everything went sideways, I'll give you that." Marion kicked off her shoes and tucked her feet underneath her. "But lots of great things happened too. You got out, you had some wine and lots of Christmas treats, we took a carriage ride!"

"I feel like I need a vacation from my vacation. I'm exhausted."

"I think we should take our minds off it. What if we had a spa day tomorrow—something fun that doesn't have anything to do with notes or the book or anything? I'll bet I could book us a couple hours at Stillwater Sanctuary. Anthony's sister has connections."

"I don't know if I'm up for it," Heather said honestly.

"Once the book is released, you might get really busy if you do end up taking Nick to court over it, and you're going to want to be rested. Tomorrow could be your last day to relax."

"I worry my head won't be in it."

"But you need to get your head back into *your* life. You can't change what's happened to you. All you can do is try to move on. Do something entirely for you this holiday."

Marion was right. Heather had gotten wrapped up in her past this Christmas, and while meeting Nick had been a setback, she couldn't hide under her covers forever. "You might be right."

"I'm always right," Marion teased. She stood up. "Now, are we eating in or out? It's dinnertime, and from the looks of you and the state of your full coffeepot over there, I'll bet you haven't eaten."

Despite all she'd been through, good things did happen for Heather, and they were all due to Marion. She couldn't have managed this season without her.

Chapter Twenty-Nine

Midday the next day, Heather found herself dressed in a white robe next to Marion at Stillwater Sanctuary. After having Chinese takeout last night, Marion had spent the evening trying to cheer her up with rom-com movies. While Heather's troubles hadn't disappeared, she had to admit Marion had lifted her spirits enough to get her through the evening.

"We're starting with herbal tea and manicures," Marion said as they walked barefoot across the natural stone floor toward a pair of cushy, high-backed chairs.

They sat down, and a woman handed them a menu. "We have teas for whatever ails you: calming and stress relief, refreshing and cleansing, warming and comforting, detox, and immune support. I'll give you a minute."

Heather squinted at the menu. "A tea for whatever ails me? I'm not sure they have a tea that would make Nick vanish." Then she waved her hands in the air. "Sorry. Focusing on the present..."

Marion snorted. "That *was* a good one." She ran her finger

down the choices. "I'd say the anti-Nick teas would be the calming and stress relief or maybe cleansing?"

"The chamomile says it helps you unwind... Or maybe passionflower? That's relaxing."

"I'd go with passionflower," Marion replied, "but that's just me."

They settled on warm cups of passionflower tea and a couple shades of red polish for their nails. Two women with crystal bowls containing warm water and lemon slices took their seats across a thin table from them and asked Heather and Marion to soak their fingertips. As the woman across from her squeezed an orange-scented scrub on the backs of Heather's hands, she tried to keep her mind empty by focusing on the experience.

Low, airy instrumental music played somewhere in the background. Apart from that, the spa was quiet, filled with soft light and muted sounds as the technician applied pressure to parts of her hand she hadn't realized were fatigued. Warm water steamed gently from the bowl, and the faint scent of lavender lingered in the space between them. She closed her eyes, taking in the feel of the woman rinsing the gritty scrub from her hands and wrapping them in a warm towel. The woman applied lotion to her skin and hit more pressure points. Then she got to work on Heather's nails.

As the manicure progressed, the atmosphere was unhurried, like a pause set apart from the holiday she'd just had. *This, too, shall pass.* The nurse who'd helped with Toby had said that at some of the hardest times, and it only came back to Heather now. She'd been so caught up in the frenzy of the holiday that she hadn't had enough quiet time to remember until this moment. Under the spell of relaxation, she told herself that the book would come out and eventually fade as the next big thing came along. Nick's type of deception would never hurt her again, because she was more informed about these things now. And, eventually, she'd get over the haunting sadness that he hadn't been the amazing guy she'd thought he was. She'd keep going, and one day, these things would have passed, and if she was lucky, she might be happy at some point. Or at least content.

Once their manicures and pedicures were finished, with sparkly toes, they headed into another location for facials. They were given a terry cloth headband and strapless wrap to wear, then went into a dark room that smelled of citrus and honey, with candles and more quiet music. They each reclined in a chair lined with comfortable blankets and the facialists got to work, massaging and working their cheekbones, necks, and temples. Heather relaxed, allowing the moment to whisk her away.

After massages and an oil-infused hair treatment and blowout, they twisted up their fresh locks and slipped on their swimsuits for their final activity—a warm soak in a large tub full of rose petals. Heather climbed in and sat next to Marion.

"This was a great idea," Heather said. "I feel like the ick from the last few days has been scrubbed off me. Thank you."

Marion smiled. "Glad I could help." She waved her hands through the rose petals. "There will be tough things in life that we can't avoid. You know that better than most. But it's how we manage through them that makes us who we are."

"Speaking of tough things, did Anthony ever say anything about the parenting book he was reading at the bookshop?"

"No, but he's been asking a lot of questions, like what makes *me* know I'm ready to have kids and how am I sure I'll be able to handle the responsibility." She ran her hands along the surface of the water, pushing the rose petals into a line. "I think he might be reconsidering, and we haven't even gone to our first therapy session yet."

"That's wonderful news."

"I don't want to get too excited, but I've never seen him this pensive about anything else."

"Toby and I wanted kids one day. We put it off so he could get a foothold in the industry, and before we could even blink, it was too late." She sank into the water until the petals were floating around her chin. "The book comes out tomorrow. Nick was pretty convincing—he had me fooled. Will he fool everyone else too? What if he sensationalizes everything?"

"Well, you have two choices: One, you can ignore it and let people think whatever is in that book is true. Or two, you can do a couple of interviews to set the record straight. At the end of the day, the truth is with you, and deep down, everyone will know that."

Marion's words sank in. She was right again. When everything was said and done, that book didn't matter to all the readers as deeply as it did to her, and while many copies would be purchased and read, the information in it would eventually become old news, and no one would care anymore.

"I still don't understand why Nick sent the letters as if he were Toby if he wasn't trying to get information from me. What if he's doing some kind of follow-up project, and he wants more material?" She sat up. "He did say he'd tell me everything tomorrow. I'm going to force him to explain that."

"Maybe you should unblock him," Marion suggested.

Heather thought back to the way his laugh had made her feel when they'd first met, the anguish on his face as she'd driven away, and the roses he'd sent yesterday. Her time with him flashed in front of her like a slideshow.

"Everything inside me wants the guy I first met on that plane. I fell for him right away, when I never thought I could love anyone again after Toby. Nick was able to derail me with his charm, and I can't forgive him for that. I also don't trust that he won't break my heart over and over again if I let him."

Marion frowned. "Yeah."

"I will need to unblock him, though, if I want to find out the whole story tomorrow."

❄

When Heather got home, still channeling her inner calm, she turned on her Christmas tree, lit a few candles, got her fluffiest blanket, and curled up on the sofa. The roses taunted her from the table across the room.

She picked up her phone and brought up her settings, then scrolled down to Blocked Contacts. Staring at the screen, a mixture of fear and longing overtook her. She was scared to let Nick call her. And if she were being truthful to herself, as she'd told Marion, she could probably still fall for his charm. His dishonesty had rocked her. Maybe that was why Toby had avoided the press. Had he known something she'd only just learned?

Tomorrow was New Year's Eve, and then she'd click over into next year. What would the New Year bring for her? She couldn't shake the fact that even with the situation with Nick, the notes had been good for her. She'd enjoyed getting the wine, spending time with Marion on the hunt, shopping in bookshops, and spending time at the cabin.

If Nick had been behind everything, he had cleaned the cabin, decorated it for Christmas, and stocked it with all the food. Why? What was he planning next? Her mind went reluctantly to the worry that he'd installed cameras or recorders. What information had he gotten while she was there? She wanted answers. Would she ever get them?

She got up and paced. Her gaze landed on her journal sitting on the desk. Nick had taken everything from her, but she decided that, starting now, he couldn't take away her conversation with Toby. She wanted to talk to Toby, and this journal—whether based in truth or not

—had been her lifeline to him. On a clean page, she wrote:

> *Dear Toby,*
>
> *Tomorrow's going to bring some pretty big changes. I have no idea how it will go, but I'm going to do my best to manage it. Just know that while I may or may not handle things well, I'm always trying to honor you with my choices.*
>
> *I love you.*

She closed the journal and set it back on the desk. Could he see everything that was going on? Had he been shouting into the void, trying to warn her? She'd never know. But maybe she could at least get a little closer to Nick's motives tomorrow. And maybe—just maybe—get some real answers.

She unblocked his number.

Chapter Thirty

Heather's phone was ringing off the hook in the living room before she'd even opened her eyes. She got up and yawned, walking into the room to see who was calling.

Nick.

"Hello?" she answered.

"You unblocked me!" Nick's euphoric voice came through.

How many times had he tried to call her? Did he have some kind of unblocking radar? It hadn't even been one night.

"It's conditional," she said, rubbing her eyes. "Tell me everything. You promised."

"I can't yet."

"What? Why? It's December 31st. I thought that's why you were calling."

"Did you get the flowers?" His voice was soft, thoughtful.

Was he trying to smooth over the fact that he was clearly stalling?

"Yes." She wasn't going to admit to him how beautiful they were or that their fragrant perfume made her house smell like a million bucks. "Look, I'm only going to entertain this call if you start explaining. Otherwise, I'm hanging up."

"Wait! Don't hang up."

She paused, irritated. If Nick was going to rouse her out of a sound sleep, he'd better talk. And fast.

"Hanging on the doorknob of your apartment is a dress and a pair of shoes. They're your size. Put them on, and I'll pick you up at six o'clock tonight. Then I'll tell you everything. Cross my heart."

"No. I'm not playing your games. Tell me now."

"It's the last thing I'll ask of you, and then you can decide whether or not you want to speak to me again."

He had her. She had to comply if she wanted to get to the bottom of all this.

"Fine." She'd do what he asked, hear him out, and then never cross paths with him again.

"All right, see you tonight," he said enthusiastically.

She hung up the phone, groaned, and rubbed her sleepy eyes. Then she immediately called Marion and told her what was going on.

"Do you need a wingman?" she asked.

"I can hold my own with Nick," she replied.

"What does the dress look like?"

"I haven't gotten it from the front door. Hang on." She peered through the peephole to make sure no one was going to jump out at her when she tried to get the dress. The coast was clear. Quickly, she opened the door, grabbed the bags, and yanked them inside, locking the bolt once more. She unzipped the garment bag and sucked in a breath. "It's a floor-length beaded red dress."

"Oh wow. What are you gonna be doing at six? Is he taking you to a New Year's Eve party?"

She huffed out a moan. "I don't plan on partying. I need quiet so he can *talk*." She opened the shoe box to find a pair of red heels. Then, suddenly, she panicked. "You don't think he's making me attend some sort of book launch for the biography, do you?" There was no way she was going to celebrate that.

"I doubt it. He knows how you feel. And it's New Year's Eve. Everyone who's going out will be wearing dresses like that tonight."

"Should I trust him?" Heather asked.

"Am I rubbing off on you? I'm usually the one to fret over your safety."

"Maybe you are. And this whole situation has opened my eyes. Not everyone is well-meaning. They don't always have my best interests at heart."

"Make sure your phone is charged and call me if you need me. Also, put some pepper spray in your bag, just in case."

"Good idea."

"At least we just had a spa day. Your red nails will look gorgeous with a beaded red gown."

"If only there was a happier occasion to wear it."

"I want all the details tomorrow," Marion said.

"You'll be the first person I call."

They got off the phone, and Heather sat on the sofa, the dress lying on the coffee table opposite her, her mind reeling. The last thing she wanted to do was go out tonight.

She grabbed the box with the pair of heels, taking one out to slip it onto her foot, when she noticed the red-and-white envelope. While she knew now that Nick had written the notes, seeing one he'd delivered hit home a little harder. She reached into the box and pulled out the envelope. Then she read the message.

I'm taking you to dinner at Marrow and Flame Chophouse. I'll be outside your apartment right at 6:00. See you tonight.

Nick

Nick's signature blurred in front of her—a final blow to her delicate heart. While she wanted nothing to do with this fancy dinner, she'd have to endure it to hear Nick out.

She'd never been to Marrow and Flame before. In the early years, it had been out of their price range, and by the time they had enough money, Toby was too well-known to feel comfortable going there. They wouldn't have had a moment's peace to eat.

Not sure what she was going to do with the rest of her day, she began with breakfast. With all the food from the cabin that Marion had brought over, she had plenty of options. She settled on chocolate chip pancakes, scrambled eggs, and mixed fruit.

As she cracked eggs into a bowl, she sifted through this holiday's events. While nothing had turned out as she thought, in a strange way, more aware now, she could finally see things more clearly. She'd face Nick head-on without the need to crumble. Whatever he had to say tonight, she was ready.

She finished making breakfast, and instead of the day dragging on, she used the time to her advantage. She found the key for the storage unit, so she could go through it in the New Year, and she pulled all Toby's contracts and read through them, highlighting term dates and contract percentages. She'd even scoured their bank account and listed Toby's favorite charities so she could continue giving to them on a yearly basis. By lunch, she'd made a list of things she wanted to get done by the end of the holiday. If anything, she'd distract herself from the outside world for the foreseeable future.

Chapter Thirty-One

Heather zipped up the beaded red dress that fit her like a glove and slipped on her heels. She'd curled her hair and pinned it into an elegant updo. Her ruby teardrop earrings, that she'd always wanted to wear but complained to Toby that she never had an occasion, were a perfect match. If only he could see them.

While getting ready for her night out, she'd fought a looming dread. It had taken her a while to define it, and when she finally did, she didn't feel any better. Deep down, she didn't want to see Nick because that adoring look in his eyes hadn't been real. It had made her feel whole, and she was afraid to see it again.

But she'd promised herself that, no matter what, she would not allow his charm to sway her. She was going to dinner tonight for two reasons only: to find out why he'd betrayed her and to hopefully stop any further projects.

She tucked her pepper spray and her lipstick into the cream-colored clutch she'd carried at the last publisher's party and slipped on her cream faux-fur coat to stay warm in the icy winter air. Then she checked the clock.

It was time.

When she got to the bottom of her apartment building, she swallowed. Through the glass window, the white Suburban was idling out front. Her heart pattered with nerves as she went outside.

Nick jumped out, ran around the SUV, and opened her door. He was clean-shaven and wearing a tuxedo that would take her breath away if she hadn't already known what he was capable of.

"Wow," he said, seemingly breathless as he looked at her.

She wasn't going to allow him to sway her with his flattery. Silently, she hiked up her dress just enough to climb in, placed the clutch in her lap, and fastened her seat belt. The SUV was clean, the leather smooth and soft to the touch.

He shut the door, ran back around to his side, and got in. As he pulled away from the curb and drove down the street, the windshield wipers moved every so often to push the light snow out of view. His spicy cologne wafted toward her, making her shiver even in her fur coat.

Being in the car with him made her feel as if she were seeing the back side of a tapestry—the knotted jumble of stitches. Before now, she'd only seen the beauty—the kind smile, the shared chuckles, the long chats over cider. But now she was in the vehicle she'd chased with Marion, the one she'd probably passed on her way to the cabin, and his secrets had been revealed.

Along the route, they passed a chain bookstore. She purposely didn't look at the lit window for fear she might see Toby's name on a display of books. She peered down at her clutch instead.

"How was your day?" he asked, glancing over.

"Fine." She wasn't going to give him the satisfaction of chitchat.

"You know, this has all been hard on me too," he said.

"But I'm not going to say anything else until I can look at you, eye to eye."

Hard on him. Hmph. How dare he play the victim? This entire fiasco was his doing. She didn't respond. She just sat, stewing in the fact that he wasn't the guy she thought he was.

They continued in silence for the rest of the ride. Nick pulled up to the restaurant and handed his keys to the valet. Then, while the attendant opened the door for her, Nick reached into the backseat and pulled out a gift bag with tissue paper and curling ribbon. She didn't even want to think about what could be in that bag. They went into the restaurant.

Inside, they checked their coats. Well-dressed diners walked past them in unhurried waves, their voices soft to match the room's elegance, while servers moved smoothly between tables, adjusting place settings and offering quiet greetings. There was a buzz of celebration in the air, but Heather had little to celebrate tonight. She felt out of place.

As the host led them to their seats, Heather took in how the low amber lighting reflected off polished wood and crisp white tablecloths. The scent of searing meats, seafood, and buttered herbs lingered in the air, and jazz floated above the steady murmur of conversation.

Heather sat down, and once she was settled, Nick placed the bag on the floor beside his chair and sat across from her. The host filled their water glasses from a linen-wrapped bottle, then placed a narrow wood-backed drinks menu on each of their plates and left them to look it over as a candle flickered between them.

It was quite an odd atmosphere for a discreet confrontation, but there they were.

"What looks good to you?" Nick asked over his menu, his gaze lingering on her a little too long.

Does it matter? "I'm not sure," she said. She didn't know

how to be cordial with the person who was actively ruining her holiday.

She peered at the wine and spirits list, deciding. Martini, Negroni, Blackberry Bourbon, Champagne Cocktail with sugar cube and bitters, and under "lighter refreshment," her choice would be between the Elderflower Spritz and the Cucumber Gimlet.

Their waiter approached the table with a friendly smile, resting his hands at his sides. "Good evening, and welcome," he said, his cadence expertly practiced. "May I start you off with something to drink?" He glanced between them briefly before continuing. "We have our selection of classic cocktails and an extensive wine list, but we do have a few seasonal specials if you'd like me to tell you those."

"I think I've decided already," Heather said, wanting to get this show on the road. "I'll have the Elderflower Spritz."

"Excellent choice. And for you, sir?"

"I'll have the Smoked Old-Fashioned and then a soda to follow."

"Perfect." The waiter gathered their cocktail menus. "I'll return with some fresh bread."

"Thank you," Heather said.

When the waiter left, Nick's emerald eyes landed on her. "You look incredible tonight. I hope to make you feel just as incredible."

"I'm not sure you could ever make me feel *incredible*," she said.

His features shifted downward, as if her comment had been an invisible stab, and she felt guilty for snapping at him. But should she? He was certainly great at mind games.

The waiter returned with a steaming basket of buttery rolls and two dinner menus.

"Your drinks will be up shortly. I'll give you a few minutes to look over the main course options."

Wanting to get dinner out of the way so she could hear Nick out and head home, she scanned the choices. Dry-aged rib eye, filet mignon, and Wagyu, were the standouts of beef, and from the seafood options, there was butter-poached lobster tail, pan-seared sea bass, jumbo lump crab cakes...

She was still considering when the waiter brought their drinks to the table. Her Elderflower Spritz shimmered pale gold in a tall, stemmed glass, tiny bubbles rising steadily to the surface. A delicate twist of lemon and a fresh mint sprig floated on top. In front of Nick, the waiter placed the Smoked Old-Fashioned in a short, heavy glass, the beverage swirling around a single ice cube with a thin orange peel curled on the rim.

"I'll give you a few minutes to enjoy these," he said before leaving them once more.

Heather was dying to flag him down, give him their orders, and ask for the check so they could leave as soon as she'd gotten her answers, but she had to endure this little dance of etiquette instead. It was exhausting.

She picked up her drink and sucked down a large gulp. It was light and aromatic. The floral sweetness of elderflower liqueur softened the crisp prosecco. She'd need a lot of it to get through this evening.

Chapter Thirty-Two

Heather had devoured a crab cake and was now on her second Elderflower Spritz. Finally, after declining dessert, with the bill on the table, she and Nick had been left alone, the empty plates between them. Dinner had been awkward, since Nick had wanted to talk after they ate. So she'd hurried through her meal to get to the end of it.

Nick paid the bill and slipped the pen back into the leather folder.

"The dinner was a gift from me to say I'm sorry to have upset you. But I suppose you just want answers," he said, leaning on the table with his forearms. "And I can't tell you how relieved I am to finally give them to you."

She stared at him skeptically.

He lifted his soda to his lips and took a long drink, then swallowed. "To understand it all, I have to start at the beginning."

"That's the best place to start," she said.

His chest filled with air, and he looked at her for a moment, that fondness for her showing.

She didn't trust it.

"You asked who the anonymous donor was. I can tell you now." He set down his drink. "It was Toby."

Heather drew back. Did he really think she'd buy that? She was clearly wasting her time. She should throw her napkin on the table and walk out. But that strength she'd been building came back. She wasn't going to leave that easily. She'd stay to defend Toby.

"You're lying. Toby always kept things private, and he did *not* want his life story out there. He told me so himself."

"You're right. He wanted his regular life and death to remain private." He looked thoughtful. He took in another breath. "The May before last, I got a call from Toby. I hadn't spoken to him since college—Belmont, remember?"

Okay, he had her attention.

"He told me he'd been asking around to see if anyone knew someone who could write his story for him, but not just anyone. He didn't trust someone he didn't know. A mutual friend gave him my number, and he remembered me from college. I gave him a ride home from the library on campus once when his car wouldn't start."

Her hands trembled in her lap as she tried to discern whether Nick was being truthful. He was so convincing.

"He asked to meet me in a park in East Nashville—somewhere no one would notice us. We wore our gym clothes and took a walk together. He told me about his cancer and that he guessed he didn't have long before he'd be very sick. He even predicted he'd be gone by Christmas."

"He wasn't too far off. It was January," she said, blinking away tears.

Nick nodded, his own eyes becoming glassy. He cleared his throat. "Toby asked if I'd write his story. I told him that I wasn't very practiced in biographies, but he had faith in me. We met secretly, when he still felt well, and then later, when he got really sick, I came to him while you were at work. While we met at your apartment, he felt comfortable enough to tell me how worried he was about *you*. He wanted to protect you in all this, and he knew he couldn't keep from breaking your heart when he finally left us."

She took her cloth napkin from her lap and dabbed her eyes, trying not to make a scene.

"Because we were working daily on his story, he trusted me. He started sorting things, bringing me documents for safekeeping. He asked if I'd handle the rest of the renovations and finishing up the cabin until you were ready."

She'd had no idea Toby hadn't finished the renovations.

"One day, he sat me down and said, 'I can't keep meeting. It takes too much out of me.' I could see the fear in his eyes. That day, he asked me if I'd take care of you. He told me to keep an eye on you and, maybe one day, even introduce myself and make friends with you. He started telling me all these stories about you, and that was when he hatched the idea for this Christmas. By the time we'd begun to execute it, he was too sick to write the notes himself, so he asked me to do it. He said he promised you he'd come back to see you if he could, and this was his way of doing that."

It was the last thing Nick said that told her he wasn't lying.

"But why a biography? He didn't want that out there."

Nick placed the bag on the table and slid it toward her. "Open it."

She pulled the tissue paper from the top and set it beside her. Then she reached in and pulled out a thin book. The title was *Christmas With You*.

"This biography is his love story—to you."

She stared at him, tears filling her eyes.

"Toby got another of our friends to publish it. His name's Ricky Edison. He owns a very small publishing company called Iron Pen Creative. That's who I met with in

Greenville. He lives there. During my conversations with Toby and Ricky, Toby talked about how he wanted to present the book to you. He decided that you'd need a year or so to get through the worst of your grief and by Christmas, you'd deserve a little magic. We'd send you the notes throughout the holiday, and he wanted you to get the biography right on New Year's Eve, to start your next year with all his messages. So he came up with all this to show you just how much he loved you and to help you start to move forward."

She wiped her tears and, with a shaky hand, took a sip of her water to steady herself.

Nick leaned in. "I tried to call you once and invite you to the music awards in May, thinking that if we planned the event together, we could get to know each other, and it wouldn't be so weird sneaking around doing things for you. But you weren't having it."

She smiled through her tears. "Sorry."

He chuckled thoughtfully. "When you started figuring things out, I had no idea what to do. Toby was adamant that I do this on New Year's Eve. He'd worked so hard to plan it precisely. Could I have told you two days ago? Maybe. But I'd promised Toby I wouldn't. I was terrified the whole time that I'd messed this up for him."

"I'm so sorry I didn't believe you," she said, her words broken.

"You're a tough cookie," he said fondly. "Even Toby's perfect plan hasn't worked exactly as it should have. You outsmarted him."

She broke into a smile at that.

Then she looked down at the book. The cover's background was of rustic wood, with a picture of Toby's guitar and one of his writing notebooks front and center, a few pieces of balled-up paper at the sides. The title on the wood-colored cover was in a handwritten, slightly rustic font: *Christmas With You: A Real-Life Story of Love and Hope*.

"I helped him write it, but it's all from him. It's about how much your quiet strength meant to him and how he'd planned for your happiness in life and in death."

She sucked in a jagged breath. "So this is in stores?"

"No. Toby said he promised you that you'd get that choice. This is an advanced copy. Ricky's willing to change anything you don't love. You get the first look. And then, only if *you* want to publish it, we will. You have Toby's blessing."

She thought back to the day Toby's first note had shown up. She'd considered what she wanted this Christmas at the start of her vacation. She'd told herself that day that she wanted a little of Toby to show up, but she also wanted to be happy. In true Toby form, he'd managed to give her both this Christmas. All the way from heaven.

Toby's last message had said, "While you might think it's the end, it's just the beginning." And he'd told Nick to take care of her. Toby wouldn't have given that task to just anyone. Could he have been thinking of her future, knowing that maybe if she let herself, she could fall for someone like Nick?

She looked over the flickering candlelight at him. He'd done all this for her and Toby. "Thank you," she said in a whisper as she pulled the book to her chest.

"You're welcome."

She put the book back into the bag and stuffed the tissue paper on top, now wishing she hadn't rushed through dinner. "What are you doing tonight for New Year's Eve?" she asked.

"This."

"Want to ring in the New Year with me?"

He gave her a definitive, "Yes."

She clutched her bag and rose. He put his napkin on the table and stood up, then came around to her side and took the handles of the gift bag for her, carrying it to get their coats.

He'd traveled all over the place, planting those notes for her. *Who does that for someone?* The memory came to mind of him chasing after her car. He'd yelled out, "I adore you!"

Little did he know—because she had a terrible way of showing it—she felt just the same about him. Suddenly, she wanted to go back and do all the things she'd done this holiday—the wine shop, the cabin, the carriage rides, the bookshops—with him by her side. He'd been in the wings, quietly working to give her the best holiday anyone could ever ask for. And he adored her.

He stopped just before they got to the coat check. "What are you thinking about?" he asked, searching her face.

She looked up at him. "You."

Interest flashed. "What about me?"

"That I don't want to wait for midnight."

"For what?"

"This." She reached up and put her arms around his neck, closed her eyes, and pressed her lips gently to his.

Suddenly, his strong arms were around her, holding her. His lips were on hers, his spicy scent overwhelming her. The world around them faded away, leaving only the warmth and quiet intensity of their connection. A shiver ran through her, an electric mix of nervousness and longing, and when they pulled back slightly, their eyes met with shy smiles, knowing something had quietly, irrevocably shifted between them.

Welcome to the beginning, she thought. And she couldn't wait to see the next chapter.

Epilogue

The Next Christmas

"Thank you for coming," Heather said to Alice Beckmeyer from Stargate Publishing.

"I wouldn't miss this for the world."

Nick and Heather had planned the book launch for *Christmas With You* during the holiday, and it was as if the season itself had paused to remember Toby. Evergreen garlands framed the small, makeshift stage area of the local Nashville bookshop, and the scent of pine mingled with coffee and paperback books as country music fans gathered to view Toby's memorabilia and personal photos of him and Heather. His fans were many—some in pressed denim jackets, others clutching photos of him and copies of his biography—all of them taking their seats for her speech.

Though he'd been gone for almost two years, Toby's presence felt close tonight, stitched into every story and photograph, every quiet nod from those who had enjoyed his songs.

Heather stood at the podium in her green velvet holiday dress, steady, the book resting in her hands, her full journal in front of her so she could pull out a few stories to tell. Her last note to Toby was dated right after New Year's. She'd thanked him for introducing her to Nick and for his blessing.

"Thank you for coming tonight." Her voice echoed through the room.

Nick winked at her from the front row.

"I know Toby better than anyone, and when I read this for the first time, I cried the whole way through because of its absolutely raw honesty and transparency about how he felt about me. While he did a great job of telling me he loved me, I could only truly understand the depths of his love after reading this."

She went on to speak of Christmas mornings spent in a van when they couldn't afford a tour bus, of handwritten lyrics tucked into coat pockets, of the man behind the music who never stopped believing in simple truths and fighting for those less fortunate. Nick came up to read the first chapter and tell a few stories about writing with Toby. Then they stepped down into the crowd to celebrate with them.

As she and Nick signed copies of the book, Marion and Anthony passed out singles of "Highway 40" from Toby's new album. In Toby's memory, multiple artists had agreed to cut all the unpublished songs, with the proceeds going to Toby's charities: a safehouse for women, a nationwide homeless food kitchen, a music program for underprivileged youth, and one for cancer research that Heather had chosen.

Pre-sale copies of Toby's biography sold enough to launch Iron Pen Creative into the stratosphere, and Ricky scrambled to print the massive number of copies needed to fulfill all the orders. The biography hit number one the week it was announced, and Toby's song of the same name topped the charts for another year, along with a couple songs from the new album. The book and charity album were a fantastic culmination of Toby's talent.

As the night went on, Heather lingered with each person,

listening as much as she spoke, feeling as if this release were not a farewell but a homecoming. "Christmas With You" played softly in the background, along with Toby's other songs, and a couple of the artists surprised the fans with a special appearance.

When the event finished and they'd said their goodbyes, Marion, the final guest, gave Heather a big squeeze with one arm, her daughter Sadie in the other. "I'm proud of you, girl!"

"Thanks."

"Now it's time to really celebrate." She did a little dance, pulling Anthony by the arm and making Heather giggle. "I've got Sadie's and Scarlett's things and the wine packed! We're sleep-deprived and needing some adult interaction!"

Marion and Anthony's daughter was two months old. It hadn't taken Anthony too long last Christmas to come around, and within a couple months, Marion had danced into the school library and inconspicuously opened her handbag to reveal a positive pregnancy test. They'd danced through the aisles of bookshelves.

"You know the new door code to the cabin?" Heather asked.

"Yep. Got it in my phone."

"Okay, we'll see you there." Heather gave her another squeeze and then hugged Anthony.

After they left, Nick pulled Heather into his arms in the middle of the bookstore as the staff busily rearranged chairs and cleaned up from the event. "You were wonderful tonight."

"Thank you. You were too. Everyone seems to love this book."

"How could they not? It's all about you."

She pushed herself up on her tiptoes and kissed him.

He pulled back and looked down at her, his smile reaching his eyes. "Ready to go to the cabin for two whole weeks of Christmas fun?"

She wound her fingers through his. “Yes.”

“Earlier this month, while you were at work, I drove up there and decorated it for Christmas.”

“You did?”

“It was a lot easier this year since I wasn’t darting around bushes every time I heard a car on the road.”

She laughed.

“I’ve got everything packed. We just have to swing by my house and pick up Ophelia.”

“Marion and Anthony are on the way now. Think Ophelia and Scarlett will get along?”

He made a face. “There’s only one way to find out. If not, I packed Ophelia’s favorite peanut-butter bone.”

Heather laughed. “She’ll ignore everyone for that.”

Heather and Nick had been inseparable over the last year. He got along famously with Marion and Anthony, and she’d even met a bunch of his friends in East Nashville. She’d realized pretty quickly that Ophelia actually loved her when she wasn’t stomping around the house yelling, and the dog would beg her for cuddles every time they were together.

❄

The four-hour drive was full of radio Christmas carols, old stories, and laughter. The drive would have been less than four hours, but Ophelia kept crying to do her business, and they’d pull over, but most of the time she just wanted to play in the snow, so they let her.

When they finally arrived at the cabin, Ophelia jumped out and ran circles around the outdoor Christmas tree, barking and eating snow.

“Sadie’s asleep, and I’ve already got the wine poured!” Marion called from the open front door as Nick unloaded their luggage and Ophelia’s crate.

All of them were still dressed in their clothes from the launch, and the night felt festive. Heather grabbed what she could and brought it inside where Marion traded her for a glass of chardonnay. Scarlett sat in the chair by the back door, licking her paw.

Anthony had the fire going, and the candles lit, but something else pulled Heather's attention. The entire room was filled with helium balloons and there were photos tied to the end of each string. She took hold of one of the photos. It was of her and Nick ice-skating a couple of months ago. Every single photo was of the two of them—their summer ice-cream dates, candlelit dinners, her birthday, washing the car, wearing matching sweaters with Ophelia...

"What is all this?"

The dog ran in and sat on the rug next to the fireplace, and Scarlett darted to higher ground, opting for the windowsill. Nick shut the door and left the bags by the stairs.

With a smile, Marion stepped aside to let Nick walk in.

"You like?" he said.

"I love it, but you didn't have to do all this."

"Over the last few months, I gathered all our memories. I thought I'd display them so you could see what's in my head every day. I can't stop thinking about you."

She drank him in. He was so handsome in his suit, with that gorgeous look in his eyes. If Marion and Anthony weren't looking on, she'd have grabbed him right there in the living room and laid a big wet kiss on him, but she'd spare them the spectacle. Instead, she gave him her flirtiest look that said, *You'll get that big kiss later*.

But the silliness stopped when, all of a sudden, he reached into his pocket and got down on one knee. "Heather, I want more balloons. I want enough to fill an entire cathedral. I want to make memories with you for the rest of our lives. Marry me."

So much for later.

She threw herself on him and nearly knocked him over with the biggest, longest kiss. He wrapped his arms around her and kissed her back as Marion and Anthony cheered. Ophelia barked and jumped up on them, her tail wagging furiously as if she knew what was going on.

When they finally slowed, he pulled back. "So that's a yes?"

"Yes!" she said with tears in her eyes.

He slid a two-carat diamond solitaire onto her finger. Ophelia hopped around and darted to the rug to get her bone. She brought it over, her tail thumping the floor as she sat with it in her mouth.

"So much for the wine!" Marion said. "Now I know why you had the champagne in the fridge. I'll get us all some."

That night, after the champagne was poured and the toasts were made, they all changed into more comfortable clothes and settled in by the fire, chatting and enjoying each other as the balloons floated above them. Heather had to wonder if Toby had somehow had a hand in her forever after all. She felt as if he were looking down on them, cheering them on.

Toby Hart's Christmas With You

Long before the spotlight, back when my dream of writing songs was fragile and mostly unspoken, much of my attention was spent on a young woman who caught my eye at a bar. She was way out of my league, the most gorgeous copper-brown eyes and dark hair. I'd had just enough alcohol to give me the courage to talk to her. Then, something amazing happened. I made her laugh. It sounded the way I'd imagine heaven to sound. I knew right then that she'd be a problem for me because I wouldn't be able to think about anything else.

I was right. Long after the alcohol had worn off the next morning, I still couldn't get her smile out of my mind. It haunted me. That night, instead of asking her to get out her phone, I'd scratched down my number on a beer mat, took the rest of the night to gather enough courage, and quickly shoved it into her hand on my way out the door. She'd tucked it into her purse, where I guessed she'd keep it until she got home, where she could safely trash it.

I couldn't believe she'd given me the time of day as it was, but on a Saturday morning, she actually called, so I asked her over to my cramped apartment, where I strummed a borrowed guitar because it sounded better than mine, and created a few lines to impress her.

Next thing I knew, she was in my passenger seat, coming home on a late-night drive from a bar gig where the pay barely covered gas. In that quiet beginning, she was already there—a steady presence in my life.

Needless to say, I hurried up and married her.

She was working extra shifts, packing lunches, reminding me why I'd started whenever doubt crept in. My love story with Heather and the story of my songwriting were never separate.

In the early days, when my schedule was all over the place, through missed holidays, uncertain rent, and the emotional weight of believing in something no one else could yet, Heather was by my side. She listened to half-finished songs at the kitchen table, offered honest feedback, and celebrated the smallest wins as if they were gold records. Before fame, before the publishing contracts, before success, she was there—and everything that followed stood on that foundation.

I knew then that I would give her my entire life. And if I could find a way to give her more than that, I would...

A Letter from Jenny

Hello!

Thank you so much for picking up my novel, *Postmarked December*. I hope it made you optimistic that miracles can happen this holiday season.

If you'd like to know when my next book is out, you can **sign up for my newsletter here:**

https://www.itsjennyhale.com/email-signup

I won't share your information with anyone else, and I'll only email you a quick message whenever new books come out or go on sale.

If you enjoyed *Postmarked December*, I'd be so thankful if you'd write a review of the book online. It's one of the biggest gifts you could give me.

Speaking of gifts, I've included a book club reading guide and some delectable recipes. I hope you enjoy them!

Until next time,
Jenny

Book Club Reading Guide

What's better than a festive December day? Christmas is such a busy season, full of activities and opportunities to spend time with loved ones. A holiday book club or a quiet day in with a good friend during this season would be perfect to discuss *Postmarked December*. The mistletoe, glittering trees, and celebratory atmosphere, along with a room full of holiday treats and maybe even a fire, would be a wonderful backdrop for a cozy meeting among friends.

Grab your favorite fuzzy sweater, woolly socks, and comfy jeans and, while you're doing that, get ready to enjoy great conversation. Here are a few questions to get you talking, and an array of delicious recipes from the novel that would be a perfect complement to your book club.

1. Which character do you relate to most and why?
2. Would you have followed the notes to see where they lead, as Heather did? Why or why not?
3. How do you think Heather handled the situations with Nick in the novel? Was there anything you think she should have done differently?

4. Could you imagine an alternate ending for this novel? If so, what would it be?
5. Were there any moments in the novel that surprised you? If so, what were they?
6. What scene in the novel was the most uplifting for you?
7. How might this story impact your own life?

Toby's Sugar Cookies —As Sweet As Heather

- 1 cup softened butter (leave on counter for 45 minutes to an hour beforehand)
- 2/3 cup granulated sugar (plus a little extra for topping)
- 2 cups all-purpose flour
- 1 teaspoon vanilla
- 1 small glass (for flattening dough)

In a medium bowl, beat together butter and sugar until combined. Add in flour and vanilla and blend well. Make small dough balls in your hands (about the size of a golf ball) by rolling and kneading them until they are smooth, sprinkle with sugar, and place the balls on a greased baking sheet. Press the bottom of the glass onto the ball to flatten it into a cookie shape. Bake at 325°F for 14–16 minutes. Let cool and enjoy.

Toby's Famous Marshmallow Fudge

- 3 cups raw sugar
- 3/4 cup unsalted butter
- 2/3 cup evaporated milk
- 2 cups semi-sweet chocolate chips
- 1 seven-ounce jar marshmallow creme
- 1 teaspoon vanilla extract
- 1 cup chopped walnuts or almonds
- candy thermometer

In a saucepan, bring sugar, butter, and milk to a boil, stirring continuously. Once boiling, continue stirring for about 3–4 minutes. Using a candy thermometer to measure the temperature of the fudge, remove saucepan from heat when mixture reaches 230°F. Add in chocolate, vanilla, and marshmallow creme. Mix until melted. Then add in walnuts or almonds. Line a 9 x 13 inch baking pan with foil and grease with butter, then pour in mixture. Let it cool overnight. You may want to chill in the refrigerator to get it firmer.

Golden Elderflower Spritz

Makes one glass.

- 1 1/2 ounces elderflower liqueur
- 2 ounces premium dry prosecco
- 1 ounce sparkling mineral water
- 1/4 ounce fresh lemon juice
- 1 thin lemon twist
- 1 small mint sprig
- 2–3 ice cubes

Fill a large cocktail glass with the ice cubes. Pour in the elderflower liqueur and fresh lemon juice. Gently stir to combine. Add the prosecco slowly, then top with sparkling water. Give a very light stir to mix layers without flattening the fizz. Garnish with a lemon twist resting on the rim and a mint sprig tucked beside it.

About the Author

Jenny Hale is a *USA Today*, Amazon, and international bestselling author of romantic contemporary fiction. With over a million copies sold, her books are available worldwide, translated into multiple languages, and have been adapted for television.

The Beach House, released in 2021, sailed to number three on the Amazon US Kindle chart, and *The Magic of Sea Glass*, an Amazon US Kindle chart topper, was a 2024 gold medal winner in the Independent Book Publisher Awards. Two of her novels, *Coming Home for Christmas* and *Christmas Wishes and Mistletoe Kisses*, have been adapted into Hallmark Channel original movies.

Her stories are chock-full of feel-good romance and overflowing with warm settings, great friends, and family. Jenny is at work on her next novel, delighted to bring even more heartwarming stories to her readers. When she isn't writing or heading up her romantic fiction imprint, Harpeth Road, she can be found running around her hometown of Nashville with her husband, two boys, and their labradoodle, taking pictures—her favorite pastime.

Acknowledgments

To Oliver Rhodes, I am so thankful for the potential you saw in me at the very beginning and the time you spent teaching me the business of writing. Your strong example also paved the way for my journey into publishing. I will not let a book go by without first thanking you.

To the editors of this novel: To Megan McKeever, I am so thankful to have had your input on the plotlines. You have such a strong eye. Lara Simpson, thank you for making absolute magic out of this book with your line edits, as always. Kendra Olson, you are fabulous. Thank you for all your hard work on this novel. Lauren Finger, thank you for shining this story up and getting it ready for a crop of new readers. I'm so happy to have had your eyes on the final version. To my cover designer, Kristen Ingebretson, you are the best of the best! You take my crazy ideas and bring them to life.

And last of all, a heartfelt thank-you must go out to my husband, Justin, and my kids for being so supportive as I pop into a room, fist pumping and shouting, "I got my daily 1,000 words!" You are an amazing support and my whole world.